The van immediately reversed, tires squealing.

Raising his weapon, Gabe fired at the van's panels, emptying his rounds at the same time Mac began to fire. The front window imploded.

Nice shot, Mac.

The vehicle did a three-point turn and raced out of the parking lot, melting into the night.

Standing, Gabe dusted gravel from his pants. He inspected the torn elbow of his blazer. His knee protested loudly; he was getting too old for gymnastics in a parking lot.

"That's twice you've saved my life," Mac said. Her steps were unsteady, the limp more pronounced as she continued toward him with the dog in tow.

"Do I get points for that?" Gabe's hand trembled with the last traces of adrenaline as he plucked a blade of grass and a bit of gravel from her hair.

"I'll let you know," she said.

A slight smile crossed Mac's face. Exertion had warmed her skin to pink. Despite the disheveled hair and the abrasion on her chin, for the first time since he'd arrived on her doorstep, she seemed truly alive.

Tina Radcliffe has been dreaming and scribbling for years. Originally from Western New York, she left home for a tour of duty with the US Army Security Agency stationed in Augsburg, Germany, and ended up in Tulsa, Oklahoma. Her past careers include certified oncology RN, library cataloger and pharmacy clerk. She recently moved from Denver, Colorado, to the Phoenix, Arizona, area, where she writes heartwarming and fun inspirational romance.

Books by Tina Radcliffe

Love Inspired Suspense

Sabotaged Mission

Love Inspired

Hearts of Oklahoma

Finding the Road Home
Ready to Trust
His Holiday Prayer
The Cowgirl's Sacrifice

Big Heart Ranch

Claiming Her Cowboy
Falling for the Cowgirl
Christmas with the Cowboy
Her Last Chance Cowboy

Visit the Author Profile page at LoveInspired.com for more titles.

SABOTAGED MISSION

TINA RADCLIFFE

LOVE INSPIRED SUSPENSE
INSPIRATIONAL ROMANCE

LOVE INSPIRED® SUSPENSE
INSPIRATIONAL ROMANCE

ISBN-13: 978-1-335-58789-3

Recycling programs
for this product may
not exist in your area.

Sabotaged Mission

Copyright © 2022 by Tina M. Radcliffe

All rights reserved. No part of this book may be used or reproduced in any manner whatsoever without written permission except in the case of brief quotations embodied in critical articles and reviews.

This is a work of fiction. Names, characters, places and incidents are either the product of the author's imagination or are used fictitiously. Any resemblance to actual persons, living or dead, businesses, companies, events or locales is entirely coincidental.

For questions and comments about the quality of this book, please contact us at CustomerService@Harlequin.com.

Love Inspired
22 Adelaide St. West, 41st Floor
Toronto, Ontario M5H 4E3, Canada
www.LoveInspired.com

Printed in U.S.A.

But they that wait upon the Lord
shall renew their strength; they shall mount up with
wings as eagles; they shall run, and not be weary;
and they shall walk, and not faint.
—*Isaiah* 40:31

Dedicated to the many encouraging writers
who helped birth the original concept for this book
years ago, including Vince Mooney, Rhonda Starnes,
Connie Queen, Terri Weldon, Jackie Layton,
Sharee Stover and Stephanie Dees.
It really does take a village.

To Tom Radcliffe, who kept asking if I was ever going to
write that suspense book. A huge thank-you
goes out to my deadline buddies, Melanie Dickerson
and Josee Telfer, for early morning
writing accountability sessions (really early, it turns out,
because I'm in Arizona).

Thank you to my editor, Dina Davis, for this opportunity
and my agent, Jessica Alvarez, for her support.

ONE

Winston growled, the feral sound low and drawn out, then it morphed into a snapping bark. The bulldog's barking continued, loud enough to nearly drown out the banging on the front door.

Mackenzie Sharp grabbed the Glock from the coffee table long before it registered that she'd fallen asleep on the couch again. She glanced at her watch and tensed.

It was well after 10:00 p.m. on a Friday night.

Whoever was at the door had guts. They kept knocking, and Winston kept barking. The dog was in a frenzy now, his nails clicking on the tiled floor as he raced back and forth.

"Winston. Come."

The cacophony immediately ceased. The animal crossed the living room to her.

"Good boy." She praised him as he shoved his nose against her shoulder and licked her cheek. The animal's fierce devotion had only increased since she'd returned from the CIA assignment that nearly claimed her life.

Mac slowly sat up. Gripping the handle of her ebony cane, she stood and grimaced at the stab of intense pain that shot down her left leg. She wiped a bead of sweat from her forehead.

Flying into action was no longer an option. Instead, she methodically tucked the Glock she kept for protection into the waistband of her jeans and hobbled to the door.

"No more than I can handle," she muttered. "Wasn't that our deal, Lord?"

She pulled up the security cam on her phone to assess her visitor. Framed by the silhouette of a huge palm tree that filled the horizon and backlit by the haze of a full moon, the man on her stoop faced the street.

When he turned toward the camera, she gasped.

Gabe Denton, a mistake from her past. From the days when she'd foolishly believed she could have a normal life. One that included a relationship.

Despite her careful attempts to stay off the grid, trouble had found her. He stood on her doorstep in a dark suit and tie that screamed "government-issue." Mac released a groan.

She disarmed the security system, turned the dead bolt and withdrew her Glock. When she cracked the door as far as the chain allowed, the hot, dry, desert breeze seemed to whisper as it moved past.

Fully aware that the screen door and chain lock were all that stood between her and the man on her stoop, Mac leveled the gun at her visitor and slid her index finger into position. Meanwhile, Winston nosed his way into the doorway. The muscular animal bared his teeth, all too eager to reach out and touch.

Unfazed, Denton's gaze flicked to Winston and then met hers and held. Black-framed glasses emphasized hazel irises that were warm like honey, with flecks of forest green. They offered something she hadn't expected.

Compassion.

"Hello, Mac."

Mac shivered. His voice, both smooth and husky at the same time, stirred memories she thought had been buried five years ago. "What are you doing here?"

"Shipman sent me," he said.

CIA Senior Officer Todd Shipman. Her boss and handler on the Toronto mission that had gone so very wrong.

Mac frowned, confused. Gabe Denton was a close friend and protégé of Shipman. The presence of this particular man meant something serious was going down.

"How did you even find me?" she finally asked.

He didn't answer, but his expression said that if he could find her, anyone could. Anyone. Like the unknown shooter who slid through her memory in flashes that kept her awake at night.

"I'm not operational. Shipman is well aware of my status," she continued.

"He hoped you'd make an exception."

"An exception? To what? Shipman decommissioned the task force. Which leaves me unassigned as well." Lips clamped tight, she met his gaze again. She wouldn't address the obvious physical limitations that kept her from returning to the Agency anytime soon.

He looked past her into the house. "May I come in?"

Mac didn't try to hide her frustration as she released the chain, opened the solid metal door and then the screen, careful not to lose her balance.

As he moved past her, his jacket inched back, revealing a leather shoulder holster and a SIG Sauer. Mac tensed at the sight. Sent by Shipman and carrying a weapon? It certainly was not protocol.

Denton stared pointedly at the gun that still targeted his upper torso. She tucked away her own weapon as he stepped into the room and looked around. He frowned and evaluated her living space, leaving no doubt that he was as thrilled with her generic rental as he was with being here.

That made two of them.

Hiding out in suburbia was not part of her planned career path. Nor had she expected to find herself in the middle of a mission that had gone south. The assignment eight weeks ago had left her injured and her fellow agent Liz Morrow presumed dead.

The physical healing from Mac's injuries was slow. Her mental and emotional healing even slower. Mac had finally reached the other side and was able to sleep a few restless hours at a time. She'd been on her way to becoming whole again. But all that had been destroyed when she'd been compromised by an unknown gunman at the rehab facility. She'd left her condo in Denver and arrived at this rental two weeks ago to try yet again to get back on her feet, literally and figuratively.

Now this man's arrival threatened to toss every scrap of that hard-won progress out the window.

"Off the beaten path, isn't it?" he commented.

Mac shrugged. That was the point. The place sat on a cul-de-sac on the edge of the desert, along with six other identical one-story stucco homes with red-tiled roofs. The grounds consisted of decorative gravel and cacti. Spartan. Like the inside. Cell service could be counted on to be spotty, but traffic at this end of the residential development was nil. All good, since she was trying to be inconspicuous.

Mac leaned back against the closed door and released a long breath. "Why are you here?"

Denton shoved his hands in his pockets and faced her. He was silent for a moment, as if deciding how much information to share. Mac couldn't help but assess him. Nothing had changed. Gabe Denton still looked good in his nerdy *GQ* kind of way.

He cleared his throat. "There's a situation, and Shipman needs you."

"The man has an entire organization at his disposal," she said.

"He wants you."

And that sealed the deal. Mac couldn't and wouldn't refuse her boss. Even Denton knew that. They went way back. Todd Shipman had been her father's best friend. The Shipmans had taken her under their wing when she was fifteen—the year her parents died.

Still, Mac had made the decision to go to ground, locking out even Shipman, in a last-ditch effort to keep herself alive.

Yes, she'd do anything for the man, but in her current condition, her assistance on an assignment would be more a hindrance than a help.

The look in his eyes since Denton had stepped into her home said he agreed.

"If you expect me to leave Phoenix, you're going to have to do better than that," she said. "I had protection in Denver, and that didn't stop someone from trying to put a bullet in me." She paused. "Or should I say, another bullet?"

Denton offered a short nod that let her know he was well aware of why she'd fled Colorado.

"The Agency has intel that Elizabeth Morrow is alive and being held hostage."

"What?" Mac's stomach took a hit, and her knees threatened to buckle. She gripped her cane tightly.

Liz was alive? Goose bumps shot up her arms.

For eight weeks she had been grieving the loss of her partner on the mission. Grieving and heaping guilt upon herself for Liz's death.

Mac worked to calm the rapid beating of her heart. "I assume they're acting on that intel." She barely got the words past her trembling lips.

"The intel is being verified. In the meantime, Shipman feels that the threat to your personal safety has escalated and he wants you to come in."

"You said he needs me. This is a different story." Mac shook her head. "Thanks, but no. I've done a pretty good job keeping myself alive up to now."

"He wants you to come in." The words were resolute, his gaze unwavering.

Dread washed over Mac. She swallowed. "I'm going to need more. Who has Morrow?" This time her words were barely a whisper as she shoved back the fear that nearly strangled her.

"I don't have that information."

"Someone has Liz," she murmured, the words unbelievable.

Then she did the math. Eight weeks. Where had Liz been all this time? Mac shook her head, clearing away the images and questions slamming into her. If only she could figure out why the Toronto mission went sideways and why she was on someone's hit list, she might be able to get ahead of the situation. Thus far, she had no clue, and to her knowledge, neither did the Agency.

"There's a plane waiting for us at Sky Harbor," Denton continued. "From there, we'll head to the Denver office, where Shipman is waiting to brief you."

Mac nodded slowly again, digesting the information. Liz was alive.

She was afraid to be relieved. Her mind swirled as her gaze narrowed to focus on Denton and his plan to take her to Denver International Airport.

"Okay. Now we know why me," she said. "Why you?"

"He trusts me." Denton paused. "And he hoped that you would, too."

She stared at him for a moment, sorting her thoughts. Of course Shipman would use her history with Denton as leverage to gain an advantage. While they hadn't parted on contentious terms, the current situation was nothing less than awkward.

"Then you can read me in," Mac finally said. She'd prefer to get the details from her boss, but the sooner she could begin processing, the better.

"My job is to get you to Denver. Period."

Not surprised at his response, Mac offered an annoyed grunt. Gabe Denton was a letter-of-the-law sort of guy. If he did know more than he'd let on, he wouldn't break protocol.

"Fine. I'll get my ready bag and Winston's supplies." She was only agreeing because Todd Shipman had made the request. Not because she wanted or needed the Agency's protection.

Denton's gaze went from the dog to her. His expression said he wasn't pleased.

That wasn't her problem. The bulldog would make up for the fact that she wasn't functioning at 100 percent yet. He'd also have her back. Because until the assailant who'd put half a dozen bullets in her in Toronto and tried again in Denver was found, she didn't trust anyone else to keep her alive. Not even Gabe.

Gabe Denton did his best to keep his face impassive. Though he tried not to show concern, he couldn't deny an unexpected surge of protective emotions when he looked at Mac. She'd lost at least ten pounds since he'd seen her last, and the haunting blue eyes were underlined with dark smudges, indicating she slept little, if at all. But there was something else, besides lack of sleep. Mac was functioning by rote. The spark that used to be in her eyes was gone.

While they hadn't kept in touch since their breakup five years ago, he'd made a point of subtly asking about her whenever he met with Shipman. There was something about Mac that touched him in a way that no one else ever had. He hadn't realized he'd had a heart until she'd broken it.

Gabe had read her file before he left Colorado. It was filled with heavy redactions regarding her disastrous assignment in Canada. Removed from the duty roster for postoperative recovery in Denver, she'd been compromised at the facility where she'd been receiving outpatient rehab. The agent assigned to protect her had been shot and killed.

Mac had gone to ground. He'd have done the same thing. The Agency was tasked to protect its operations officers. What went wrong?

Guilt tore at him. He should have visited her in the hospital, but he'd been convinced she would refuse to see him. Mac loathed anyone, especially him, seeing her vulnerable. As it was, she was less than happy to find him on her doorstep tonight.

He shook his head. What was Todd Shipman thinking? And why had Gabe agreed to be the liaison for this mission? Right now he ought to be fly-fishing in Montana. So why wasn't he?

Because Shipman said that with the uncertain intel on Liz, Mac would be safer if she came in, and he was sure that Denton could convince her to come back to Denver. Then there was the fact that Denton owed Shipman his life and his career. So, yeah, agreeing was a no-brainer.

As he walked around the small living room, his gaze fell on a framed photo facedown on the coffee table. Gabe flipped it over. It was a younger and markedly less thin Mac standing with her parents, smiling at the camera. He'd seen the picture of her parents before, though she had never talked about the embassy bombing that had left Ambassador and Mrs. Sharp dead.

He'd lost his own mother to cancer since he'd last seen Mac. The fact that he and Mac had a lot in common failed to comfort him. Two loners recruited into government service, living lives that were lies for the greater good.

About once a year, he considered a line of work in the private sector.

Once this assignment was complete, he vowed to seriously give a career change more thought. He found himself shaking his head.

Who was he kidding? He was a company man, and he probably always would be, if only to keep his father happy.

When Mac returned to the room, her chin-length straight blond hair had been tucked behind her ears, mostly hidden by a black ball cap. A cane was in one hand and a black duffle in the other. She'd strapped a messenger bag across her chest. Again, he noted the dark circles around her eyes and the awkward movements.

He was headed on a mission with a woman who was in no way ready for the field. Dread left a sour taste in his mouth.

As if reading his mind, she lifted her face in challenge.

For a moment, he stared, more than a little intrigued by the proud tilt of her chin and the fire in her eyes. She was a beautiful woman, despite her current issues. Almost unconsciously, he stepped back. Yeah, and he'd been burned by Mac once before. He still cared, and that was a dangerous thing.

"How's the leg?" he asked. "You had surgery?"

She nodded. "A bullet tore a chunk of muscle from my hip. They grafted replacement tissue from…elsewhere and put a metal rod in my lower left leg, where another bullet fractured the tibia." She raised an eyebrow. "Any other questions?"

Denton eyed the bulldog with concern. "Can I trust that he's not going to take a piece of me?"

She patted the animal's head. "You never were a dog person, as I recall."

"Nope. Never had a dog." Dogs were complications, and his father, the general, didn't do complications.

"Winston's bark is much worse than his bite," she said.

"If you say so." He glanced around the room. "What kind of dog is he?"

"American bulldog."

"And does he have a crate?"

"He prefers a harness."

Gabe opened his mouth and closed it again. Great. Just great. The fact was, now he was escorting two bulldogs to Denver.

He opened the front door and assessed the cul-de-sac's perimeter while Mac dropped her bag to clamp a leash on the dog. The brown-and-white animal trotted out the door, eager for an adventure. Though his owner stood in the open doorway digging in her messenger bag, Winston kept moving down the paved walk.

His leash continued to stretch until the dog suddenly stopped and stiffened. Winston stood on the edge of the walk, staring across the gravel yard to the curb, at the black Yukon that Gabe had rented at the airport. Ears perked, tail raised, Winston offered a low menacing growl.

Gabe froze.

The hair on the back of his neck stood up.

His gut said to get away from the vehicle.

In a split second, his brain agreed.

"Back! Get back in the house!" He grabbed the dog's leash and yanked hard to get Mac's attention. Eyes wide, she complied and pulled Winston toward her.

Gabe glanced over his shoulder in the same second that the vehicle exploded. He raised his arms to protect his head.

The bright light of a fireball turned the darkness into day. Shrapnel and glass flew, accompanied by a deafening boom that ripped the night.

There was no way to escape the wall of heated force that slammed into him. Gabe flew through the air toward the house. A painful jolt resonated down to his bones as his body thudded into the frame of the screen door, and he slid to the warm cement.

Car alarms sounded for a few moments.

Then nothing.

Silence.

With a hand, he pushed himself to a half-sitting position.

Whoa. Dizzy.

His head spun, and he collapsed back down to the ground. Gabe stared at the sky, mesmerized by fragments of the wreckage that floated through the air. A hot ember shot into the darkness, glowing like a fiery ruby.

When something warm and wet touched his face, Gabe jerked back. Turning his head, he met the bulldog's concerned eyes.

Then he assessed the house. The aluminum door had crumpled with the impact of his body. The dog stood inside, his head poking through the flaps of the torn screen.

Mac? His heart clutched with desperation as he tried to look around.

Where was she?

Gabe called her name. The words registered as a dull, muffled sound. Almost as if he was underwater.

Once again, he called out.

Then he stopped and fell back to the cement.

He couldn't hear.

Couldn't hear and wasn't certain if Mac was dead or alive.

Lord, help us, he prayed.

TWO

Mac blinked and refocused. She was lying on the tiled floor of the entryway. With a groan, she rolled to her side and sat up, trying to make sense of what just happened.

"Winston?" Panic choked her as she searched for the bulldog. "Winston!"

The dog barked. He raised his head from where he stood with his body halfway through what was left of the mangled screen door.

Mac picked up her cane and struggled to a standing position as realization hit. Denton had pushed her and Winston back into the house. He'd saved their lives.

On the other side of the door, Gabe Denton lay motionless. Mac worked to slow the quick, shallow breaths that accompanied her racing heart. Though she willed herself to focus and tried to push back emotions, she couldn't get past the sight before her.

"No. No. No. Not Gabe. Please, not Gabe," she whispered on an agonized breath.

Metal on metal screeched as she used her shoulder to bend the doorframe far enough out of the way to get to him.

Stepping outside, behind the cover of a large bougainvillea bush, Mac gasped at the sight of the smoldering metal that used to be a black SUV. The thick, acrid odor of burning oil and melted rubber hung in the air.

Her hands shook as she eased to the ground and placed her fingers against Denton's carotid artery. His pulse was strong and regular.

Relief surged through her.

There was no way she could take responsibility for another death. Especially not this man. She'd ended their relationship so this wouldn't happen.

"Denton?"

When he didn't respond, she spoke louder. "Denton!"

He moved his head a fraction and groaned.

Nothing had ever sounded so good. For a moment, Mac closed her eyes and said a prayer of thanks.

Then, she assessed the scene around her, grateful that the vehicle had been parked at the curb of the cul-de-sac, between her house and the empty one next door, and not in her drive. Heated embers from the explosion sizzled on the ground around what used to be the SUV.

Across the street, a few unknown elderly neighbors gathered, clutching their bathrobes closed. They stared and whispered beneath the streetlamps, yet didn't dare move closer. Most of the houses were empty, waiting for the snowbirds who would return to Phoenix in late autumn.

Mac carefully scanned the area, but saw nothing amiss. The desert beyond the houses remained dark, with a few regal saguaro cacti visible in the distance.

Someone had triggered the explosive on the SUV from afar. In the desert, perhaps? Were they still watching? A shiver ran over her at the thought.

Mac took a deep breath before assessing Denton for injuries. The cuts and scratches on his face were superficial. If those were the worst of his injuries, the man was fortunate. No doubt his shoulder was bruised from plowing into her door, and she could only pray there were no serious internal injuries.

When she ran her fingers over the lump at the back of his head, he opened his eyes and winced. He was in pain. But he was alive.

Ignoring the fire that shot up her leg, she staggered to a standing position once more and froze. The wail of emergency vehicles echoed in the distance, getting closer and closer.

"We have to get out of here," she murmured. If

not, they'd be caught up in bureaucratic red tape for hours instead of heading to Denver.

Denton groaned again, his lids drifting closed. Beneath the glow of house lights, his skin reflected an eerie pallor.

Take him with her or leave him here? Could she trust him? The question hammered at her, along with a dozen more. Had she been targeted, or had he? It was unlikely he'd set a device that harmed himself, yet…

Her mind raced with possible scenarios. Not one of them was good and her concerns escalated. There was a fine line between suspicion and paranoia. She was letting fear take over instead of her training.

Mac took a deep breath, and in a split second, the decision was made. Denton was coming with her. But caution prevailed, so she reached into his jacket and took his service weapon.

Denton's eyes popped open, and his hand shot out to circle her wrist. His gaze moved from her face to the SIG Sauer in her hand.

"Easy," Mac murmured. She pulled out of his grip and put the weapon in her messenger bag.

Jaw clenched, Denton grimaced and moved to a sitting position.

"Are you okay?" she asked.

He didn't answer. Instead, he palmed the ground until he found his glasses in the gravel.

After straightening the bent frames, he slid them on his face.

"Denton? Are you okay?" She said the words louder this time.

He turned to her, head cocked, confusion on his face. "Say something." His words were spoken much louder than necessary.

"You saved my life," Mac returned.

"I can't hear you." He cupped a hand to his ear.

"How...about...now?" She enunciated with exaggerated slowness, her voice as loud as his.

"That's better, except you sound like you're underwater and far, far away." He offered another grimace as he shifted position.

"Are you okay?" Mac repeated.

"Your house hit me."

She nearly laughed aloud at the comment and the crooked smile that transformed his face into the endearing man from so long ago.

Except there was nothing amusing about the situation.

Yet, when he met her gaze and something connected between them, she paused at the humor that lurked in the depths of the hazel eyes.

Lighten up, Mac. It was as if he'd said the words aloud. Like he had so many times in the past.

She forced herself to look away. "Do you have any idea who did this?" she asked.

"Not a clue."

She should believe him—after all, he'd been injured. But once again, paranoia whispered in her ear and told her not to take anything at face value.

Denton stood and then suddenly swayed. Mac stepped toward him, and he grabbed her arm.

"Careful there." Thoughts whirling, she continued to evaluate him.

Possible concussion, with hearing impairment and vertigo. She'd seen auditory fatigue in the field. No way were they flying to Denver until his ears had recovered. The shift in air pressure driving to the higher elevation would be painful enough. Flying? Out of the question. It could permanently damage his hearing.

"Call Shipman," Denton said. "He'll extract us."

"No. I'm not calling anyone yet."

"Why not?" He asked the question with his eyes fixed on her mouth, obviously reading her lips.

Mac didn't answer. She didn't tell him that she'd been putting together theories since the events in Toronto and Denver. Little things that didn't add up. She'd managed to stay alive in the past by trusting her gut. That's exactly what she'd do now. She would stay far away from the Agency until she was certain of whom she could trust.

Once again, she pushed back the twisted metal of the screen door with her shoulder, so both of them could get inside the house. Out of habit, Mac locked the dead bolt behind them.

"Let's go." She picked up her bags and cane, then faced her dog. "Winston. Come!"

"Where?" Denton asked. He leaned against the couch, as if steadying himself.

"Denver." She nodded toward the kitchen. Dropping what was in her hands, she grabbed a bag of dog food and took her keys from the wall.

Mac opened the door to the garage. A nondescript 1997 navy Crown Victoria gleamed in the half light. She opened the trunk and tossed in the dog food before grabbing a case of plastic water bottles from the shelf behind her. Attempting the transfer without putting weight on her leg proved more difficult than expected.

Denton appeared behind her. He took the water from her hands and shoved the pack into the trunk.

"Thanks." She reached for an emergency-medical-supply tackle box from the shelf and slid it onto the floor of the front passenger seat.

Turning to Denton, she spoke slowly. "How's the head?"

"Sore."

"First-aid kit is in the front seat. Get in the car."

He stopped her with a hand on her arm. "We need to talk."

When she stared at his fingers circling her arm, he released her and stepped away.

"Sorry."

"We can talk in the car." Mac headed to the kitchen, slammed supplies into an insulated tote and picked up her ready bag. When she returned to the garage, Denton stood in her path.

"You're driving to Denver?" he asked.

"That's right. You can't fly. You'll permanently damage your ears." She took off her messenger bag and placed it and her ready bag behind the driver's seat. "You've had a noise-induced threshold shift. Hopefully temporary," she added. "Winston! Come!"

The dog rushed into the garage at her command, his leash trailing behind. A red plastic food dish was gripped between his teeth.

"He's done this before," Denton observed.

Yes. She and Winston had taken drives to nowhere over the last few weeks. Long drives to help clear her head so she could think. She'd been preparing for today. The day when she'd be on the run again.

Mac removed the leash and tossed it and the food dish into the back seat. She grabbed her cane and limped to the other side, then pushed back the passenger seat. "Come."

Winston jumped in, and she fastened his harness.

Once she and Denton were settled, Mac pressed the garage-door opener. With a heavy foot on the gas, the Crown Vic shot into the cul-de-sac. She wasn't going to wait around for another explosion.

"Ouch." Denton's hand shot out to grip the dashboard. He reached for his seat belt as she made a hard right.

"Sorry." She grimaced with regret at the necessary move. Mac well knew what it was like to feel every bump in the road, and she hurt for him.

Once they'd turned the corner, she eased off the gas pedal but kept the headlights dark while directing the vehicle to an exit. Less than a minute later, a police car's flashing lights reflected between the crowded subdivisions of homes several blocks over.

"Code three," Denton murmured. He slid down in the seat.

He was correct. Law-enforcement code three indicated lights and sirens activated as a response to the emergency situation. Mac flipped on her headlights and steered into traffic, where they passed more police cars, lights flashing, headed to the neighborhood.

"We got out of there just in time," Denton said. "The last thing we need is to spend hours explaining who we work for and why."

She nodded and glanced in the rearview mirror. "We're out, and so far without a tail."

"Does anyone else know you were staying in the rental house?" Denton asked.

"No. What about the SUV?" she asked him. "Can it be traced back to you?"

"I used an Agency alias. The trail will dead-end."

Several blocks away, she slowed for a red light in front of a twenty-four-hour urgent care. The facility's name in neon heralded the entrance.

Mac glanced at her passenger and again noted his abrasions. He'd always reminded her of Clark Kent with those glasses and his perpetual shadow of stubble. Gabe had always been a good guy. Straight as an arrow and chivalrous. Had that changed? She hoped not.

For a moment, her mind wandered to five years ago.

No.

Mac gave a slight shake of her head. She couldn't—wouldn't—allow herself to think about their past. Not now. All she knew was that he didn't deserve the beating he'd taken on her account. The right thing would be to drop him here and drive to Denver alone.

Mac raised a hand and pointed toward the building as the signal changed to green.

"Not necessary," he said. "Hearing is improved."

"That's because I've been yelling. You could have internal injuries and most likely a concussion."

"Tomorrow, I'm going to hurt in places I didn't know I could hurt. As for right now…" He shrugged. "My bottom line is that Shipman said to escort you to Denver, and I'm going to do that."

"Your call." She glanced in her rearview mirror, then drove in and out of the side streets a few more times to be sure they weren't followed before hitting the on-ramp to the expressway.

"Cell-phone detonating device?" Denton asked.

She nodded. "Most likely. There are miles of desert behind the cul-de-sac. And plenty of dead zones."

"Which threw off the timing."

"That's my guess," she said. "And there's no way they'd have planned for Winston standing between me and the vehicle."

He offered a slow nod, eyes on the road, clearly deep in thought.

"How did you know?" Mac finally asked the question burning in her gut.

"The device?"

"Yes."

"God's had my back for a long time. I try to listen to what He's telling me." He paused. "Your dog's behavior outside your house only confirmed things."

God? Her gaze moved from the road to the man in her passenger seat. She'd never heard anyone at the Agency make that kind of admission, except Shipman and Denton. For the first time in a long time, she found herself without a comeback. She admired his transparency about his faith and always had.

"You've got my phone and my weapon," Denton continued.

"You don't need either at the moment. But for the record, I don't have your phone."

"I must have left it in the rental. Which means

it died in that explosion. Accounting is going to kill me. That's the third phone I've destroyed this year."

"You're alive. They'll get over it, and at least I don't have to consider that someone is tracking us using your cell." She shot a quick glance in his direction and froze. "That was presumptuous. Sorry. Is someone expecting your call?"

"Huh?"

"Wife? Girlfriend?" She raised her voice with the questions she really didn't want the answers to.

"Yeah, right. I think we already proved that this job doesn't make for sustained relationships."

"Merely asking." Mac quickly closed her mouth before she said anything else awkward. She couldn't help but recall that they'd managed a mostly long-distance relationship for nearly a year before she'd ended it. Things were mostly good, except she kept waiting for the other shoe to fall.

They were in a line of work with risks, and she couldn't handle it if someone else she cared about died. It wasn't until Gabe had left that she realized how much she already cared. That part surprised her.

"Compromised-agent protocol requires us to check in and update them on our location and status," Denton said.

"What?" Mac shot him an annoyed glance. Surely he wasn't spouting Agency regs right now.

"Comprised-agent protocol. You must have a burner phone."

"Nothing is required of me. I'm not active." She kept her eyes on the road, without mentioning the ready bag behind her seat that held not one, but two burner phones, along with everything else she needed to survive off the grid.

"You don't trust Shipman?" Gabe asked.

It was time to make herself perfectly clear. Mac turned and met his eyes in the dim light of the vehicle. "I was compromised in Toronto and then in Denver. It's in my best interest if I don't trust anyone at the Agency at this point."

"Why did you agree to go to Denver if you don't trust Shipman?"

"I owe it to Liz," she said grimly.

A few minutes later, Denton swiveled in his seat as they passed a sign pointing in the other direction, toward Flagstaff. "Where are you going?"

"Next stop is Tucson," she said loud enough to ensure that he heard her.

"Why aren't we going north?"

"We're heading to Las Cruces."

"Las Cruces!" Denton slapped a hand on the dash and stared at her. "That's an additional hour and forty-five minutes at least."

Mac leveled him with a cold stare, surprised at the uncustomary outburst. "Your ears can't handle the rapid elevation change. The drive to Las Cruces will give you a little more time to adjust."

And she hoped that anyone who decided to check the highways wouldn't consider a detour to New Mexico.

"They'll be searching for us when we don't show up at Sky Harbor Airport," Denton said.

Mac scoffed and shook her head. "That's the least of my worries."

"And what about Morrow?" he asked.

"I can't help Liz if I'm dead. Right now, the only thing that I'm certain of is that someone tried to blow me up."

"Ah, you forget that I was nearly killed, too."

"Sorry, but I'm guessing you're collateral damage to whoever is behind that explosion." She assessed him for a reaction, but he failed to deliver. "Maybe it's time you shared what you know."

"I told you. Shipman will read you in. I'm just your escort to Denver."

"Right. Stick to the script."

"Protocol," Denton muttered. "Not a script."

Silence stretched, taut with unspoken concerns.

Gabe glanced around the Crown Vic. "Whose car is this? My briefing indicates you own a hybrid."

"I bought it off of a Craigslist ad. It's a vehicle. Reliable, and it has a twenty-gallon gas tank. The Vic, like the house-rental agreement, is in the name of an alias."

"An Agency alias?"

Mac shook her head. "Let's call it my safe identity."

"Follow the rules much?" he asked.

"Nope. And that's probably why I'm still alive."

For a few minutes, she silently reviewed tonight's events in her mind. Why did she open the door to Denton? It went against all her self-preservation rules. Something automatic had kicked in when she saw his face. An emotional response based on their history that said Denton could be trusted, though she wouldn't tell him that. Now, she could only pray she hadn't made a fatal mistake.

Mac looked at him. "How did Shipman find me, anyhow?"

"Not Shipman. I found you. I remember you once joked about Phoenix in July being a great place to disappear because no one comes here in the summer. I called rental agencies and had them cross-check all the leases from around the time Shipman said you left Denver. Yours was the only one paid for in cash. Secured with a prepaid anonymous credit card under a name I was unable to trace."

Mac didn't have a response. The admission caught her off guard. There was some small pleasure in the realization that he'd remembered anything she'd said five years ago.

"You were right." Denton frowned. "It's near

midnight and has cooled down to eighty-five degrees."

Her gaze followed his to the tall shadows of saguaro cacti illuminated in the light of the full moon as they moved down the lonely stretch of highway.

Eighty-five cool degrees in Phoenix. All in all, a nice night to die.

Not if she could help it.

Gabe ran his fingers over the massive lump on the back of his head. A headache was building, and it was going to be a doozy.

Mac's gaze darted from the road to him. "You okay, Denton? You've been awfully quiet for the last hour. Not nauseated or seeing double, are you?"

"I'm fine, except for the little hammers beating my skull. Hearing is a little better, but, man, the ringing won't let up." He turned to Mac. "Got any ibuprofen?"

"Tackle box. At your feet. Ice packs are in one of those bags on the floor by Winston."

He removed a small packet with two white tablets from the tackle box and swallowed them dry, then pulled down the visor. His eyes rounded at his reflection. Dried blood had crusted on the cuts on his face, and the frames of his glasses were still ridiculously askew.

Gabe groaned. "Why didn't you tell me I look like a home-improvement project gone bad?"

"I figured alive was good enough."

He rummaged in the back seat for an ice pack and held up a rubber chew toy.

Winston barked and grabbed the toy from his hand. "Careful. I might need my fingers."

Mac smiled. "That's his favorite toy."

"No kidding. Ah…which bag has the cold pack?"

"Sorry. The brown insulated one. There are wet wipes in there as well."

After he'd swiped at the cuts on his face, Gabe twisted his glasses into place, then applied the cold pack to the back of his head.

"So it seems you have a plan. Care to share?" he asked.

"A plan? You think I have a plan?" Mac shook her head. "We're two hours away from a car explosion. I'm still trying to answer a thousand questions. How about you?"

"I'm low on plans but chock-full of questions, too. Like…oh, I don't know. Who wants you dead?"

"I don't know, either." She gave him a quick side-glance before once again focusing on the road.

Gabe nodded slowly. She didn't trust him, which was why they were both skirting around the obvious. He couldn't blame her. After eight weeks, the Agency has a lead that Morrow is alive, Mac comes out of hiding and immediately there's another attack on her life. Coincidence? Not in his line of work. What was going on? Why did they want Mac dead? And who were *they*?

He cleared his throat. "To be clear, my only mission is to get you safely to Denver."

"Right," Mac said. "Because you're Shipman's protégé."

"And you're his family," he returned. "Which is why he made me come to Phoenix."

"As in, twisted your arm?"

"Let's just say—" he paused "—I owe him a few favors."

She nodded. "As I heard it, you don't spend much time in the field anymore. You're being groomed for greater things."

Gabe didn't deny his ambitions. Instead, he pulled in a deep breath. Mac wouldn't understand. Never had. She didn't do long-range planning. In his opinion, she was afraid to think about the future.

Well, not him. He'd worked hard for his upcoming promotion. A promotion that would secure him a much-coveted permanent position at "The Farm," the Central Intelligence Agency's training facility at Camp Peary, in Virginia. It was a safe position. One that his father approved of. And Gabe refused to allow this detour to Phoenix to mess up finally securing the old man's blessing.

Silence filled every corner of the car. Gabe knew Mac well enough to realize they were both doing the same thing—trying desperately to figure out what was going on. She was asking herself questions she wouldn't pose aloud because she wasn't certain which team he was on. And that was understandable.

They'd been compromised. Could he convince her it wasn't him?

To get a sense of the bigger picture, he needed to figure out what went down with Mac's last mission and where Morrow had been for eight weeks.

Mac glanced in the rearview mirror and hit the left turn signal.

"Someone back there?" he asked.

"I'm not sure, but the left lane is in the shadows, so I'll stay there."

"What did you see?" he prompted.

"I thought I saw lights overhead. I'm probably imagining things." She glanced at the sky, and his gaze followed. "Full moon."

"I don't hear anything. Do you?" he asked. His thoughts had immediately gone to drone technology.

"No. It was a split second of light. Could have been anything."

"Anything…" he murmured. "Think any of this has to do with your last mission?" he asked. "Care to fill in the blanks on those redactions?"

She tensed, her jaw tight. "You read my file?"

"Sure I did. You'd do the same."

"I'd like to see your file."

"Come on, Mac. I'm an open book," Gabe said with a shrug. "As always." He couldn't resist the dig. The wedge between them five years ago had intensified because Mac couldn't and wouldn't let down her guard. It seemed the song and lyrics hadn't changed much. Her walls remained erect.

"Why are we going to Denver instead of DC?" she asked.

"Shipman's been working in the National Resources Division in Denver." He resisted adding that she'd have known that if she'd checked in.

Mac blinked as if trying to wrap her head around the information. "You mean since the rehab-facility incident?"

Gabe nodded. "Yeah, he rented a house in Cherry Creek. Since the kids are both in college, he decided to get out of DC and give this try."

"He never mentioned that," she said.

"You haven't checked in since you left rehab. Shipman's been concerned." An understatement. Shipman had moved mountains to determine who was behind the attacks on Mac.

"Why Denver?" she asked, ignoring his comment.

"Why not?" Gabe said. "There are more foreign operatives than ever in the US, and Denver is centrally located. The perfect location for a domestic unit." That was the truth. It was also the truth that Shipman wanted to be close to Mac's home base.

"What about you?" she asked. "When was your last field assignment?"

"Two years ago."

"Two years!" She shook her head. "We're in big trouble."

"What do you mean?"

"You're out of touch, and I'm out of commission."

Gabe bit back a rebuttal. She was right and it stung. He'd been in various training classrooms around the country for the last two years, including his current stint at Camp Peary. Hiding. Just like Mac, though he hadn't realized it until now.

"Good thing I brought Winston along," Mac said.

At the sound of his name, the dog barked and put his paws on the console between the seats.

"Is he hungry or something?" Gabe asked.

Mac checked her watch. "Or something. He needs to take a walk."

Gabe groaned. "The clock is ticking, and we're taking doggy potty breaks?"

She pointed to the green sign on the right of the highway. "We're thirty minutes from Tucson. We can stop at a nice clean rest stop."

"A gas station?" Gabe asked.

"No. A rest stop. Restrooms, vending machines and a parking lot."

He frowned and gave a slow shake of his head as red flags waved wildly. "I don't know if that's a good idea."

"It'll be fine. They're well lit for travelers."

"Yeah, great," Gabe said. "Good lighting, so we're better targets."

Mac reached into the back seat and pulled out his weapon. "Here you go. Thirteen rounds should be plenty for any unforeseen circumstances while Winston does his duty. Right?"

"He's your dog. You tell me."

"If it makes you feel any better, I need to stop as well."

Gabe slipped his weapon back into his shoulder holster. "I guess this means you do trust me."

"I'm being practical. If you're here to eliminate me, go ahead and get it over with. If not, then I expect you to cover me."

He released a loud breath of frustration. "Relax, Mac. We're on the same team."

"Denton—"

"Gabe."

"Look, *Gabe*, I've simply learned not to expect anything from anyone."

"I see nothing much has changed in five years." He shook his head. "That's a depressing attitude."

Mac's blue eyes faltered for a moment at his response. Then her chin rose. "My attitude has served me well."

"Has it?" Gabe paused at her words, knowing

she was in serious denial. "Have you considered reckless optimism instead? It seems to work for me."

"There's nothing to be optimistic about."

Her words saddened him, and he struggled to respond. "Look, all I'm saying is that maybe you need to step outside of yourself and look at the world from someone else's point of view."

"What's that supposed to mean?"

"It's not all about you, Mac. Shipman's not exactly sleeping at night knowing you're in danger and he hasn't been able to keep you safe."

When her face paled, he realized she had no clue. "He said that?" she asked.

"Not in so many words. I think we can agree that the guy isn't real warm and fuzzy. Not unlike you."

Mac's eyes flashed and she stiffened.

"There are people who care for you, Mac. Letting them in makes you vulnerable. I get that. But, right now, it might be the only thing standing between you and the barrel of an unknown enemy's gun."

THREE

Gabe kept his eye on Mac as she limped across the parking lot with her cane in one hand, the leash in the other, and the messenger bag across her chest. Winston led the way, trotting cheerfully toward the flat stucco restrooms surrounded by gravel landscaping. He supposed he should be grateful that the parking area was empty of other vehicles and they were safe for the moment.

Once she was out of earshot, Gabe dug in her ready bag and grabbed a burner phone. He turned the volume up, before punching in Todd Shipman's secure and private line. No doubt about it, once Mac found out what he was up to, she wouldn't be happy.

"Where are you? And what happened?" Shipman barked. "The Phoenix field office notified me of the explosion two hours ago."

"That was fast," Gabe said.

"Local law enforcement traced the vehicle's

VIN back to the rental agency and your alias, setting off the usual red-flag alerts."

"We just pulled into a rest stop outside of Tucson." Gabe glanced at the road they'd just exited. Only the odd car zipped by on the highway that ran parallel to the isolated rest area. The night had cooled even more, down to a tolerable mid-seventy range.

"Why are you driving?"

"I can't fly. The explosion affected my ears, and she refuses to leave me."

"Is she hurt?"

"No. Mac and the dog are fine."

"She brought the dog with her?" Shipman paused. "Of course she did. Nothing else to do with a dog in the middle of the night, I suppose. And that animal is closer to her than any human."

"I guess you've met Winston?"

"Yeah. A few years ago." Shipman released a frustrated breath. "A bulldog. There's some irony," he muttered.

Gabe could envision his boss shaking his head. Despite Shipman's gruff exterior, the man held a soft spot for Mac.

"Does Mackenzie know anything?" Shipman asked. "Has she said anything?"

"Sir, with all due respect, I'm confused. What is it you think she knows? The woman plays her cards close. I have no idea what she's thinking."

"Find out. That's why I sent you down there."

That's why I sent you down there.

Was it? The comment gave Gabe pause, but he didn't challenge Shipman. Didn't ask the obvious. What was going on? He'd been given enough information to prep him for the trip, but hadn't been given read-in privileges on the big picture. Gabe bit back his own frustration and worked to remain calm. This was supposed to be a protective detail. Clearly, there was more to this mission.

Instead, he asked, "Any intelligence on the explosion?"

"Our people have taken over the scene, but processing will, of course, take weeks. The neighbors reported seeing you and Sharp flee the area."

"Where will that lead?"

"No need to shout. I can hear you," Shipman said.

"Sorry about that," Gabe said, lowering his voice.

"We've already sanitized the situation," Shipman said. "The follow-up will be a few lines buried in the *Arizona Republic* about a faulty electrical system in the vehicle."

Gabe opened the car door and stepped out, praying Mac couldn't see the phone or hear him talking. He continued to move in a slow clockwise circle to assess the perimeter.

The small rest area was mostly gravel with palm trees and spiny-stemmed succulent plants.

At the end of the parking lot, a pergola with a red-tiled roof protected a picnic table.

"What's your ETA to Denver?" Shipman asked.

"Twelve hours."

"Twelve hours!"

"Yes, sir." He paused. "Has there been any further intel on Morrow? Have you been able to verify proof of life? Was the voice on the phone recorded or live?"

"I have nothing I can share at this time."

Gabe's jaw clenched at the confirmation of his greatest fear. "Who knew that I was coming to Phoenix?" he asked.

There was a beat of silence. "If there was a leak," Shipman said, "I'll run it down. That's all I can say right now."

If? Gabe opened his mouth to protest and stopped. What was going on here?

There was something else. He could hear it in Shipman's voice, and though he'd been with the Agency long enough to understand "need to know," it outraged him that there were layers to the situation that he wasn't privy to even though it could very well compromise the safety of the woman he'd been sent to protect.

"Anything else, sir?" Gabe asked.

"Ahh…" Shipman hedged. "As a matter of fact, there is a small problem."

"You can trust me, sir."

"I know I can. I'm just not sure you need this

information right now." Shipman paused and released a breath of disgust. "We've received intel on Mackenzie as well. If true, it makes her complicit in the Toronto bank job."

Stunned by the words, Gabe glanced over at the building she'd disappeared into. There was no way Mac was involved. No way. Both he and Shipman knew that if she was a suspect, she'd been set up.

"Just bring her in, Gabe. I'm counting on you to keep Mackenzie safe so we can sort this out," Shipman said.

"Yes, sir." This time the words were a numb response. As he leaned into the car to stick the phone back into the duffle bag, squealing tires signaled a vehicle approaching.

When Gabe jerked up, his head made a solid connection with the doorframe. "Because I need another lump," he muttered as he slid his hand into his jacket to retrieve his weapon.

A black Ford panel van raced through the rest-stop parking lot, bouncing over the speed bumps. Gabe did a quick assessment. There wasn't a distinguishing thing about the vehicle. Windows in the front only. No plates. No other markings. It looked as if it had been stolen straight off the dealer's new-car lot.

In a heartbeat, the van picked up speed and headed right toward Mac where she stood outside the restroom building.

And she wasn't moving.

Winston whined and tugged on the leash while Mac stood on the sidewalk staring at the van, her face ashen beneath the overhead lights.

"Move, Mac," Gabe yelled. "Move." Could she hear him above the noise of the vehicle?

A frantic Winston barked and again yanked on the leash until she grabbed the dog and dove behind the restroom building, her cane tumbling to the pavement mere seconds before a spray of bullets echoed in repetition.

Someone dressed in black held an AR-15 and stretched out of the passenger window.

They were targeting Mac. Did they realize he was on the scene as well?

Flashes burst from the muzzle like mini explosions as rounds were emptied. Gabe's gut clenched.

Distraction. He needed to create a distraction. It was the only way to save Mac.

He counted to himself, waiting for an inevitable pause after thirty rounds. Except there was none, which meant an aftermarket magazine.

Mac was pinned by a weapon that could hold up to one hundred rounds.

As quickly as the thought raced through his mind, the firing stopped, and the distinct sound of a jammed weapon could be heard. The van stopped moving.

Reload ammo. Their mess-up was his advantage.

Gabe crouched down and approached the van,

remaining in the vehicle's blind spot. Raising his weapon, he aimed for the passenger-side mirror.

Boom! The mirror and mounting shattered into pieces.

The van immediately reversed, tires squealing.

He dove to the ground and rolled out of the way behind a trash receptacle as Mac advanced toward the retreating vehicle. Raising his weapon, Gabe fired at the van's panels, emptying his rounds, at the same time Mac began to fire. The front window imploded.

Nice shot, Mac.

The vehicle did a three-point turn and raced out of the parking lot, melting into the night.

Standing, Gabe dusted gravel from his pants. He inspected the torn elbow of his blazer. His knee protested loudly that he was getting too old for gymnastics in a parking lot.

"That's twice you've saved my life," Mac said. Her steps were unsteady, the limp more pronounced as she continued toward him with the dog in tow.

"Do I get points for that?" Gabe's hand trembled with the last traces of adrenaline as he plucked a blade of grass and a bit of gravel from her hair.

"I'll let you know," she said.

A slight smile crossed Mac's face. Exertion had warmed her skin to pink. Despite the disheveled hair and the abrasion on her chin, for the first time since he'd arrived on her doorstep, she seemed truly alive.

Gabe averted his eyes and crouched down to give Winston a good rub behind the ears. "You did good, Lassie," he crooned.

Winston sat on his haunches, tail wagging and tongue hanging from the side of his mouth.

"I'm the target," Mac said. A statement, not a question. Her gaze moved to Gabe. "You need to get out of here while you can."

Gabe cocked his head and stared for a moment, thoroughly annoyed at her words. "Maybe you need to read my lips." He paused. "I'm not leaving you."

"Very honorable and completely unnecessary."

"Yeah?" He chuckled and put his weapon away. "Mind telling me why you froze back there?"

Mac stared out in the direction of the highway. Her face transformed, as if a curtain had been pulled. The blue eyes became dull and vacant. She licked her lips. "I thought I recognized the guy holding the rifle."

"Who?"

"The shooter from Toronto."

"You're sure?" Gabe swallowed, unease increasing in direct proportion to the headache beginning behind his eyes.

"No." Mac ran a hand over her face. "I'm not sure of anything. It's dark, and it happened so fast."

The questions kept coming, faster than he could analyze what was going on.

The only thing he knew for certain was that

Mac had no business being here. She wasn't ready. Another misstep and one or both of them might pay the price, and they both knew it.

"Where's your cap?" he grumbled, working to remain impassive in front of Mac.

She waved a dismissive hand in the air, and her shoulders slumped as if a cloak of emotional exhaustion overtook her. "Somewhere…"

Gabe slowly headed back to the restroom building, assessing the exterior damage as he walked. The black ball cap was lying on the sidewalk next to the decorative gravel. It was only by the grace of God that it wasn't Mackenzie Sharp he was picking up off the ground.

Burning anger ripped through Gabe at the destruction. For the first time in his life, he questioned the directives of Todd Shipman. What was he thinking? Mac should be in a safe house right now. Gabe couldn't accept the wisdom of putting her out in the line of fire if there was a leak at the Agency.

Was it part of proving her loyalty to the CIA? Making sure she hadn't turned? Both ideas only added to his ire.

Gabe scooped up her cap and strode to the vending machines. Reaching in his pocket, he pulled out a dozen coins and shoved them in the machine. The candy bar caught on the metal curl, refusing to drop. He gave the machine a vicious kick. A half dozen or so chocolate bars were re-

leased. With a hat full of candy, he headed back
to the car, just as several vehicles pulled into the
rest area.

"We've got to get out of here before someone
asks why that building is filled with bullet holes."
He met her eyes. "You have anything in your vehicle besides dog food?"

"What is this for?" She stared at the bars in
the cap, confusion on her face. "Hypoglycemia?"

"Reflexive anger." He nodded toward the car.
"I'm asking about firearms. Do you have anything
besides your Glock?"

Gabe tossed her a candy bar, and she caught
the package with one hand.

"Sure," she said. "I have a few flash-bangs and
assorted toys."

"This information would have been good earlier. We move our line of defense to the inside of
the car."

Mac nodded and stepped to the trunk.

"Oh," he continued. "And I'm driving."

She whirled around, indignant. "It's my car."

"It's my life."

They stood toe-to-toe for a few moments, Mac's
eyes locked on his. She would never back down.
He'd have to appeal to her common sense.

"Look, like it or not, we're partners now. We
have twelve hours to Denver. You're of no use to
me as a backup without rest."

"Denver? I'll be fortunate to make it to the state

line at this rate. And I don't need rest. What I need is to figure out what's going on. Now."

"We'll figure it out. Together." Gabe paused. Who would have thought when this day started that he'd be saying those words to Mackenzie Sharp? Not him.

"You landed on your leg," he continued. "It's got to be killing you. Take some aspirin and let me drive."

"Okay. Fine," she muttered, finally standing down.

"That's the spirit." He shoved the chocolate in his blazer pocket and handed her back the ball cap. "Hey, Mac?"

"Yes?"

"You and the dog are...finished?"

"We are."

"Good. Because we won't be stopping at any other nice, clean rest stops." Gabe met her gaze. "I'm going to get you to Denver, Mac. Alive. I will keep you alive."

Gabe released a breath, praying that he hadn't just made a promise he couldn't keep.

Mac sat straight up in the passenger seat. How had she missed what was right in front of her? She shook her head and looked over at Denton. "Pull over."

"Why? We're right outside of Las Cruces." He glanced at his watch. "Once we hit Albuquerque,

I'm thinking breakfast. All I've had since yesterday morning is chocolate bars and pretzels from the airplane."

"I need you to pull over now, Denton."

"Gabe. My name is Gabe."

When he turned, his intense gaze bore into her, and for a moment, Mac remembered when his name easily rolled off her tongue. She looked away. "Gabe, would you please pull over?"

"You know, you're a lot easier to get along with when you're sleeping," he muttered.

"I wasn't sleeping." The words were spoken softly. Her eyes were closed, but that was as close as she came to rest. There was no use explaining to Gabe what it was like to fear sleep and the nightmares that came in those rare times of slumber.

After he moved the vehicle off to the shoulder of the road and hit the emergency flashers, he swiveled in his seat. "What's so important?"

Mac raised her head and met his gaze straight-on. Why hadn't she put two and two together back in Phoenix? Why hadn't Gabe, for that matter?

"We've been ambushed not once but twice," she said. "How?"

"The logical conclusion is that they followed us."

Mac shook her head adamantly. She'd run through the possibilities a dozen times since Tucson. "No. I've been very careful. My guess is that you have a tracking chip on you, or there's an inside man at the Agency." She paused. "Or both."

"Inside man? Maybe. Tracking chip? Impossible." When he met her gaze, his face was void of expression, his hazel eyes shuttered.

"Think about it," she continued. "They found us in Phoenix and then in Tucson. We've been on the road now six hours and made one pit stop. But we haven't seen anything suspicious. Why not?"

"You tell me."

"Because there's no rush," she said. "They know where we are. The next time they strike, we'll be dead."

"Once again, I admire your positive attitude. However, there's a flaw in your theory." He flexed his hands. "I'm not bugged. No one has been close enough to me for that to happen."

"Look, if you aren't going to even discuss this, then I'll have no choice. I'm out of here. You're going to blink, and I'll be in the wind. Then you'll have to explain to Shipman how you lost me."

He leaned back against the seat and stared out the window with an annoyingly unconcerned expression on his face. "I found you once."

"I wasn't even trying." She exhaled. "I won't make that mistake this time."

The battle of wills ensued, and an unscalable wall of silence stretched between them. She stared at his profile for a moment and sighed. In the beginning, their covert careers had united them, along with the discovery that they shared the same interests—fly-fishing and hiking.

Things changed when she realized she was in love with Gabe. She'd distanced herself from him, like she had with the Shipmans—the very people who'd taken her in—because she was afraid. Afraid of the devastating loss that came when someone you loved was snatched away, and you thought you could have prevented it.

"Could we start from the beginning? Please, Gabe?" The gentle entreaty was a far cry from the anxiety in the pit of her stomach. "When did Shipman ask you to fly from DC to Denver?"

He looked at her and frowned. "How did you know I'm still in DC?"

"I'm good at my job." It was only curiosity that had her checking on Gabe's status every now and then. That's what she told herself.

Gabe tapped his fingers on the steering wheel and cleared his throat. "I left Washington yesterday morning. I was told to drop everything and prepare for a meeting with Shipman when I landed in Denver."

"Okay, so what happened in the meeting? Who was in the meeting?"

"Just me and Shipman. He told me about the call from whoever had Morrow."

"What exactly did they say? Did you listen to the call?"

"No. Shipman said they had Morrow. She spoke briefly to confirm that."

"Was that verified? That it really was Liz?"

"It was Morrow. Whether it was recorded or live is yet to be determined."

"And?"

"And they asked for you and said they'd be in touch."

Mac searched his face, praying for more information, but Gabe didn't give away a thing. "That's it?" she asked.

"That's it. After I told Shipman that I suspected you were in Phoenix, he had me on a plane to bring you safely to Denver."

"Safely?" Her jaw sagged as a light bulb came on. "You keep using that word, when obviously the odds are stacked against me. The Agency is using me as bait to find Liz, and whoever has her is targeting me as well."

Gabe didn't respond, but he didn't meet her gaze, either, which told her everything she'd said was spot-on. Mac crossed her arms against the invisible gut punch of reality. She stared at his profile. "Why couldn't you level with me in Phoenix?"

"Because I'm right where you are. Trying to put the pieces together. My guess is that the investigation into the mission in Toronto and the hit on you in Denver yielded information that hasn't gone vertical. Think about it. The call about Morrow is probably the only lead Shipman has had in eight weeks."

Again, a tense silence filled the vehicle. Mac's thoughts raced as she methodically put everything together. "What's the big picture here?" she asked.

"I told you. I haven't been read in, either."

"Do you think the intel is genuine?" She focused on Gabe's face, searching for any indication of what he was thinking. "Is Liz really alive?"

A tic in his jaw was the only response. "I don't know, Mac."

"Okay, okay," she said, while frantically searching for answers. "If Liz is being held… Why? And why am I being targeted?"

"I don't know that, either, Mac."

She rubbed her eyes and took a deep breath. This was a nightmare. Only she wasn't asleep. There was no way to separate the truth from an unknown plot and an endgame she had yet to figure out.

"Okay," she finally said, "so we circle back to the fact that they found us, and you're the obvious connection."

"There isn't a tracking device on me."

"If that's true, then you won't mind if we head straight to a box store, and you can toss everything. Including the holster."

"No way. Besides, that's a vintage leather holster. It's broken in. You know how many nights I've spent massaging the Italian leather with conditioner so it won't bite me?"

Mac tried not to laugh at the outrage on his face. "I'll buy you a new one." She couldn't help the tone of her voice, which clearly said he was being ridiculous.

In response, Gabe's jaw tightened. "Watch my lips. No one has bugged me."

Mac raised her palms in surrender.

A vehicle zipped past on the highway honking its horn at them. "We need to get off this shoulder." Gabe glanced at the dash clock. "We could have this conversation over eggs and toast and a large coffee. I'm thinking a cheese Danish, too. I'll buy."

When he raised his brows hopefully, Mac nearly capitulated. Then common sense took over. "Let's finish this conversation first. Can you walk back through your day before you got on the plane in Denver for Phoenix? What was different? Did you buy anything? Was anything on your person out of your sight for any amount of time?"

"I'm telling you, I'm a creature of habit. Nothing…" Gabe paused.

She sensed the moment he figured it out. "What is it?"

He slid his wallet from his jacket pocket and pulled out an ID badge attached to a lanyard with a silver clip. "I was issued a new badge in Denver yesterday."

"Who gave it to you?"

"Some tech from the IT department." He narrowed his gaze, thinking. "Couldn't tell you his name."

The card was blue, indicating a front-door employee. Not a big deal. Yet her gut told her to check closer. Heart racing, Mac reached into the first-aid tackle box.

"What are you doing?" Gabe asked.

"I've got a razor blade and tweezers in there." She took the photo identification from him and carefully pulled apart the metal. A tiny electronic square sat in the middle.

A microchip that confirmed her suspicions and validated her instincts. She'd do well to remember that when the world whispered that she was being paranoid.

"You were right." Gabe slapped the steering wheel. "The smallest I've ever seen."

"Agency technology."

"Nice of someone to borrow toys from work," Gabe said.

"I hate to mention it, but I was right. On both counts. You were bugged, which means there is obviously a mole at the Denver office."

She shook her head. A plan was already formulating in her mind. A plan that would put her back in control. At least for the moment.

"We need to purchase a used car."

"Do you have a credit card that won't raise a red flag?"

"Yes, but cash would be a better option here."

Gabe's eyes rounded. "Whoa! You're telling me that you have enough cash in your bag to buy a decent vehicle?"

She eyed him. "That's why they call it a ready bag."

"I've been doing this all wrong. Mine has extra socks." He glanced at the glowing red numbers on the dash clock again. "Can we go now?"

"Yes," Mac said. "We're three hours from Albuquerque. Let's stop there for breakfast."

"You got it." He pulled back onto the road. "Albuquerque straight ahead."

"Can you drive a little faster?" Mac asked.

"No. I'm trying to fly under the radar. We don't want to get stopped and tied up explaining who we are and risk information going out on a police radio."

"Fine, but there's flying under the radar, and there's driving like a little old lady."

A half smile lit his lips. "Maybe this would be a good time for you to tell me about your last mission."

Frustrated, Mac grabbed a bottle of water from the back seat and filled Winston's bowl before she took a long pull herself. "I thought you read my file."

"I told you. Most of the report on your mission was redacted."

She cocked her head, thinking. "Why would my report be sanitized?"

Gabe raised a hand from the steering wheel. "Because Shipman suspected there was an inside person? I don't know. You tell me."

Mac released a breath. She'd been over the details of the mission so many times that she had them memorized. Two months later, the pain of what happened and not knowing why remained an open wound, and the guilt over the collateral damage ate at her until she could barely function. An asset dead and her partner's status unknown. The awful possibilities were never far from her thoughts. Not to mention the agent who died while protecting her in rehab.

Swallowing past the emotion, Mac clutched her hands together.

"I was in Toronto to investigate a bank job that occurred two weeks prior, involving a four-man armored-car detail, consisting of three Canadians and one American with dual citizenship. The American shot the other three guards and took off with twenty million Canadian dollars. None of the guards who were shot survived. The gunman surfaced briefly in the United States, and a portion of the money was linked back to an identified sleeper cell in Denver. The bulk of the stolen money was never recovered and the guard has not been picked up yet."

"So the Agency was there because of the border issue and the possible terrorist threat?"

Mac nodded.

"Why was Morrow there?"

"We were on the same task force. She had an interest in the bank job. Some connection to another asset, though I wasn't read in on the details. Shipman approved her participation. At the time, it made sense." Mac frowned. "Now? I'm not sure of anything except that someone betrayed us all."

"What went wrong?"

"My asset was prepared to share intel on the connection between the sleeper cell and the incident in Toronto. A dead drop was scheduled for Polson Pier. Our guy made the drop and we went in. Too late, I realized it was a setup. There was bullet spray—a shooter, followed by an explosion. The asset was apparently shot after he made the drop and the intel confiscated. His body was found in the trunk of his car. Divers searched, but Liz's body was never recovered, and she was—" Mac bit back the pain "—presumed dead."

Presumed dead. Such a cold and clinical term. It was the same phrase she'd heard over and over in the news reports when the embassy was bombed. Her parents, too, were *presumed dead* until their bodies were identified in the rubble days later.

Liz was her partner on the team. Her responsibility. Mac had let her down. Deep inside, a voice whispered another accusation. *Just like you let your parents down.*

Gabe released a whoosh of air. "But if the intel is correct, she is alive," he finally said.

Was she? Mac had doubts. Doubts that made her feel guilty as well. Was the intel that Liz was alive simply a ruse to get Mac into the crosshairs of the shooter?

"If Liz is alive, then I'm back at zero. Where has she been all this time? Who's holding her and why?" She looked at him. "Why didn't they kill her, and why do they want me?"

"All good questions that need answers."

Mac nodded. "Yes. I need to get back to Denver and figure out what's going on." She paused. "I have to find Liz. I owe her that much."

"Shipman is using all available resources to locate Morrow," he said.

"They've had eight weeks. Now it's my turn."

Gabe nodded slowly, as if deep in thought. Then he turned to meet her gaze. "Can you positively ID the shooter?"

Mac froze at the question, her mouth suddenly dry and her breath stuck in her chest. "I think so." Yes, she'd seen him. As she was lying on the ground that day, pain ripping through her leg, her only thought was to find cover. When she looked up, her gaze connected with the shooter.

"Mac?" Gabe called her name, bringing her back to the moment.

"I saw him briefly when he raised his weapon to fire again. Then a police vehicle pulled onto the scene blocking his line of fire. He disappeared."

"He?" Gabe asked.

"Male, white, about six feet tall. Lean. He wore a black neck gaiter over his mouth and nose, and a black cap on his head." The words were flat while Mac fought to distance herself from the terror that remembering stirred inside of her.

"And then?"

"I found myself in a Toronto hospital, and then transferred to the States when I was stable. Someone tried to take me out in rehab, killing an agent assigned to my security detail."

Without thinking, she reached down to massage the constant aching in her left leg.

"Who knew you were still alive?"

"Shipman and the shooter." Again, she shook her head. "Nothing makes sense."

"Stop trying to figure it out alone," Gabe said. "The minute you pulled out your Glock in the parking lot was the moment we became a team." His gaze remained unwavering. "We're in this together. But you have to trust me."

Together? Mac nearly softened at the word. But was she prepared to let Gabe back into her life? Five years had passed, yet one thing hadn't changed. Bad things happened to people she cared about. She couldn't—wouldn't—take that risk.

Even if her life depended on it.

FOUR

Gabe scrutinized the outdoor patio of the busy restaurant, assessing the threat risk. Though he'd chosen a table sheltered beneath an awning, with his back to the outside wall, he couldn't relax. His gaze lingered on the door to the restaurant, where Mac had disappeared to freshen up.

So far, nothing seemed out of the ordinary, yet his gut had him on high alert since they'd pulled into Albuquerque a little while ago.

"Everything look good?" Mac slid into the seat opposite him and put her ready bag on the ground next to Winston.

"So far." Gabe picked up the black carafe and held it over her white porcelain mug. "Coffee?"

"Yes, please." She reached for a red plastic water tumbler and took a long swig.

Gabe cocked his head and assessed her. The dark circles beneath her eyes remained, and she looked like she could fall asleep on the spot. He recalled only too well the periods in his life when sleep seemed elusive, like the weeks spent at his mother's hospital bedside.

But there was something else besides lack of sleep. Mac seemed to be just going through the motions.

"You okay?" he finally asked.

Startled, she shot him a cautious glance and reached for the menu. "Why do you ask?"

"You look tired."

Surprise flickered in her eyes, telling him that she wasn't accustomed to anyone checking on her well-being.

"I'm fine," she said.

Of course she was. "Yeah? How about the chin?"

"My chin? I nearly forgot." She carefully touched the abrasion with her fingers and then looked at his face. "We're both a little beat-up, aren't we?"

Gabe chuckled. "Our server asked me if the other guy looked worse or better."

"What did you say?"

"I told her I didn't look back."

Unamused, Mac raised a brow. "What about your ears?" she asked. "The elevation of Albuquerque is about the same as Denver. Any pain?"

"Oh, there was definitely discomfort when we were climbing." He sipped his coffee and gave a nod. "But except for the occasional ringing and dizziness, everything is improved. Hearing is at sixty…seventy percent. Depends on your level of mumbling."

She straightened in her seat. *"I do not mumble."*

"Okay, mutter. You mutter."

Though Mac frowned, Gabe kept talking. "I ordered Belgian waffles and turkey bacon for you."

"Thank you." She didn't meet his gaze, instead fiddled with the menu in an apparent attempt to hide her surprise.

Did she think he'd forgotten Belgian waffles and turkey bacon? He remembered way too many things about Mackenzie Sharp. Like how she preferred her coffee strong and black. Or the fact that she had a weakness for French pastries.

"Did you order a plain chicken breast to go for Winston?" she asked. The dog perked up at the mention of his name, his gaze hopeful.

"Yeah. Though I forgot to ask if he wants dessert."

"What?" She blinked, confused.

"Joke, Mac. That was a joke."

"Right."

"Lighten up. I'm going to get through to you yet. You're alive. We'll deal with everything else in due time."

"Due time," she murmured. "I'm not even sure what that means."

Though he heard her response, Gabe frowned and stared at her lips to get his point across. "What did you say?"

Cringing, she met his gaze. "I do mumble. I'm so sorry, Gabe."

He offered a nod at the admission, trying not to smile or comment on the pink that tinged her cheeks. It was rare moments like this when she lowered the walls around her that he glimpsed the real Mac. The woman he'd fallen in love with when he was an idealistic officer.

Yeah. That wouldn't happen again.

Silence stretched between them for moments before Mac tucked strands of blond hair behind her ears and glanced around. "We need to dump that tracker," she finally said.

"Where?" He eyed the early-morning patrons. "Nothing but families on vacation and truckers. We should just destroy the thing."

"No. It's been seven hours since Tucson. Whoever is tracking us has relaxed. They're certain they have the upper hand." She toyed with the salt and pepper shakers, lining them up in a neat row. "I'll think of something creative." Her glance met his. "We also need to get you some clothes." She nodded toward the box store across the parking lot.

Gabe glanced down at his dark slacks and blazer and shook his head. "Why?"

"Look around you. How many guys are wearing blazers and ties in the middle of summer?"

"I'm guessing it's the clientele."

"I'm wearing jeans and a T-shirt, and I'm not a trucker."

"No, you are not." Gabe cleared his throat and did his best not to notice how the T-shirt hugged her lithe frame in all the right places. He glanced away just as the server approached the table with a fresh pot of coffee.

The woman picked up the carafe from the table and cocked her head. "Drained it, did you?"

"Yes, ma'am. This is good stuff," Gabe said.

"The best, in my opinion. Stop by Whispering Bean down the street, on Corrales Road. That's where we get our beans."

"I'll do that."

The server's grin widened. "Anything else I can get you, hon?"

"I think we're good," he said.

"All righty. I'll be back shortly with your order."

"Thanks, Anna," Gabe returned.

"Anna?" Mac's eyes widened. "I forgot what a people person you are."

"Guilty." Gabe shrugged. "Comes from my mom. Those Southern-hospitality roots. She never met a stranger."

"Your mother." Mac touched her fingers to her mouth, and alarm filled her gaze. "I didn't mention how sorry I am about your loss."

"Thanks." Four years had gone by, but he wasn't ready to discuss his mother's passing. He picked up the silverware wrapped in a paper napkin and unrolled it. "So… I've been thinking about your mission in Toronto," he said.

"And?"

"And I have a few questions." He leaned closer and glanced around. "Am I talking loud? I can't tell."

"You're fine."

"What about your asset?" he asked.

"What about him?"

"Any reason to believe he turned on you?"

"None. Though, at this point, anything is possible."

"Possible, yes. But we agree with certainty there's someone on the inside."

Mac offered a nod, and then grimaced as though the admission caused actual physical pain. "My asset and Liz paid the price because I didn't see it coming."

"Mac, you paid the price, too. You can't blame yourself. Someone had a game plan in place."

"My point exactly, Gabe. I missed something. Somewhere…" Her voice trailed off, and despair settled on her face.

"Don't go there," Gabe said.

"How can I not?"

He placed a hand around his mug. "Look, I get it. You spend any amount of time in this business, and eventually, everyone faces the dark place. We're trained to be survivors, loners. Then suddenly we're against the wall with no one to turn to because we wouldn't, couldn't, let anyone close."

"Yes," she breathed out, his words clearly hitting home.

"That's when faith is the foundation to fall back on," he said. "There is nothing else that remains when your life is circling the drain, and everything is out of control."

"I know you're right," Mac said. "I'm just not there yet."

Anna approached the table, balancing a tray of food. She slid Mac's waffles, which were dusted with powdered sugar, in front of her and a plate filled with sausages, toast and a large omelet in front of Gabe.

Placing syrup and coffee on the table, the cheerful woman turned to Gabe. "Your hotcakes will be out in a jiff."

"Thanks. Oh, and don't forget my friend's turkey bacon."

She snapped her fingers. "I'm sorry, hon."

"No problem," Mac said.

Once she left, Gabe bowed his head and said a silent prayer. When he raised his head, Mac's blue eyes met his before she quickly averted her gaze. Gabe frowned, trying to decipher the action. Was she surprised at his moment of prayer? Mac had struggled with her faith in the past, and he could relate. Faith was a walk in the dark and stumbling happened to everyone. Despite their history, or the reason he was escorting her to Denver, he should find a private moment to reach out and pray with her.

"What are you thinking?" Mac asked.

"Shipman," he said. "How did Shipman follow up on the mission in Toronto, after things went sideways?"

Mac carefully poured a thin stream of syrup on her waffles before looking up. "A team was sent in to evaluate the mission. But whatever the status of their investigation—" she waved a hand "—I haven't seen a report."

He arched an eyebrow. "You weren't exactly checking in, either."

"Two weeks ago, someone tried to kill me at the rehab facility in Denver. Again. A good reason not to check in."

"Here you go." Conversation paused, and they both looked up as Anna returned with Mac's bacon and another plate, stacked high with perfectly browned hotcakes. She slid the plate in front of Gabe and departed.

"You're going to eat those, too?" Mac asked.

"Absolutely. Want some?" He edged the dish across the table.

"No. But thanks."

"Eat up," he said. "Next stop, Denver."

"Denver," Mac mused.

They ate in silence for minutes, until Mac eventually sat back in her chair, apparently replete.

She emptied her coffee cup and stared out at the parking lot.

What was she thinking? He had no idea. Even five years ago, it had been impossible to gauge what went on in Mac's head.

"What are we going to do about a safe house?" she finally asked.

"I've got an idea," he said.

"An idea? Does that mean a place that the Agency doesn't know about?"

Gabe nodded with confidence, though in truth, he wasn't certain. At some point, he'd need to make a quick phone call to confirm. "It's outside of Denver. Off of I-25, past Colorado Springs." He shoved a wedge of toast into his mouth, chewed and swallowed. "Close to a great little Thai place."

"A Thai place?" Her jaw sagged at his words. "How can you be so laid-back? It's not like we're on a road trip. We're running for our lives. Correction. My life."

He gave a slow shake of his head. Some things never changed. Mac would always be the pessimist—the opposite of his optimistic nature. Five years ago, he'd been certain they could overcome their basic philosophical beliefs. Now he realized how naive he'd been.

"Here's the difference between us, Mac. I'm well aware that at any moment, we could end up as a star on the wall at Langley. I won't let that keep me from enjoying life. It's too short. We both know that." He met her gaze, and she flinched.

"Point well taken," she said. "But mission aside, you sure think about food a lot."

"Are you maligning my character?" Gabe shook his head. "Someday, I'll cook for you. I've taken a few culinary classes since the old days."

"Someday, huh?"

"You sound like you don't believe in someday, Mac."

"I don't believe in much anymore. Period."

He stared at her. The words didn't surprise him so much as they saddened him.

Mac turned her head and frowned, her gaze on the parking lot. "See that truck?"

"The black pickup?"

"Yes. It's passed the restaurant twice."

"Looking for a good parking spot? It's a busy Saturday. We had to park around the corner."

"Could be," she said. Her tone conveyed her doubt.

"Describe the vehicle."

"Black. Tinted windows. Mint condition. No passengers." Mac paused and looked around. "Do you hear that?"

"Car alarm," Gabe said.

She stood, nearly knocking over her coffee. "It's the Vic."

"Who's going to steal a car in broad daylight,

in a busy parking lot? Someone probably hit the panic button by accident."

"I installed an aftermarket alarm." She pulled a sleek cell from her messenger bag. "It sends a notification to my phone if anyone breathes on the Vic."

Gabe stared at the top-of-the-line device, a far cry from the burners she kept hidden in her ready bag. The cell in her hand was a lot smarter than any phone he'd ever been issued.

Her eyes rounded as she pressed the screen of the buzzing cell with the pad of her finger. "Come on. I was right."

Standing, Gabe tossed a generous number of bills on the table. "Let me take Winston." He nodded toward the right. "I'll go around. Whoever it is won't see me approach."

He tore across the patio with the bulldog.

Mac had been correct. Two young men, Caucasian and in their late teens or early twenties, were at the vehicle. A tall skinny kid with black jeans and a black hoodie had his head in the car, and the other stood as a lookout. The lookout gave a nervous glance around and then began to play with his phone.

"Go, Winston," Gabe urged.

The dog barked, then streaked ahead, eyes on the target.

The lookout's head jerked up, and his eyes bugged out when he saw the stout and muscular animal racing toward the car. He opened his mouth to alert his partner, but Gabe ran into him, knocking him and his phone to the ground.

The other guy was halfway in the driver's side of the Crown Vic, his head under the dash, when Winston jumped into the car and held the fabric of his hoodie between his incisors. A tug of war ensued until the man peeled off his hoodie and scrambled out of the vehicle.

Undeterred, Winston followed, eager to give chase.

"Get this dog off me," the kid screamed.

"Winston. Down," Mac called.

Gabe turned to see Mac standing steady, with her Glock trained on the scene.

The younger kid on the ground groaned and rolled over.

"Don't move," Gabe told him.

"Nylon ties in the glove box," Mac said.

"Nice," Gabe said. The woman was always prepared.

After patting them down, he attached each to a metal bar on the store's cart-return corral.

"You can't do that," the younger kid complained.

"Sure I can."

Around them, curious bystanders approached. "It's okay, folks," Gabe called out. "Store security." He flashed his identification, careful to keep his face averted, in case someone was recording the incident with their phone. The last thing he and Mac needed was to have their covers blown.

"Grab their wallets," Mac said.

"Are you robbing us?" the younger kid asked.

"Wouldn't that be justice?" Gabe said as he frisked them. He took both wallets and cell phones and handed them to her. When their gazes met, he knew they were thinking the same thing. Were these kids involved in the attack in Phoenix and outside Tucson?

Mac flipped open the first wallet and looked up at the older kid. "What were you doing in the vehicle... Darryl?"

"Looking for loose change."

She shook her head. "I hope you have a better answer, Jason."

"Some guy paid us to take the car."

"Some guy? I'm going to need more information." Gabe edged his jacket open to reveal his weapon.

"Whoa. Whoa." Jason inched away. "I'm telling you the truth. He gave us a hundred bucks. These old Crown Vics are easy to pop and hot-wire." He shrugged. "So why not?"

"So why not?" Gabe released a breath and bit back frustration. "What else did this guy say?"

"Drop the vehicle at the airport. Said he'd meet us there and give us another hundred."

"Did he say why he wanted you to jack our car?" Gabe asked.

"Said you have something of his," Darryl said.

Something of his? Gabe hadn't inspected every inch of the vehicle, but he'd seen the back seat and the trunk. There was nothing, to his knowledge.

Mac shot Gabe a glance that said she was as confused as he was before she put away her Glock and stepped closer. "What did he look like?"

"Big guy, like a bouncer, about six feet with blond hair." He looked at Gabe and frowned. "Your age, I guess. All you old guys look the same age to me."

Gabe grimaced.

"Anything else?" Mac pointedly stared down Darryl.

"Look, lady, Jas and I were just hanging out. The guy pulls up in a black pickup. One of those Ford F-150s with the fancy raptor grilles. Dude makes an offer. We're no dummies."

"Yeah. He gave us one hundred bucks, man," Jason repeated.

"Crime doesn't pay, man." Gabe put their cell phones and wallets on the ground, inches from their hands. "Here you go."

"But we can't reach them," Jason whined.

"You're smart kids. You just said so. Work for it. Then maybe you can call 911 and report a crime." Gabe pointed at the parking-lot surveillance camera overhead. "I'm sure the security footage will verify your report."

Mac released the hood of the Vic and assessed

the engine while Gabe got on the ground and inspected the undercarriage of the vehicle. They moved like a team. A trained team. Mac had his back and he had hers without a discussion. Whoever was gunning for them had just lost the advantage.

"Looks clean." He stood and dusted off his pants.

"Here as well." Mac shook her head. "I don't get it. What could I have that someone wants?"

"I don't understand, either," Gabe said. What had Shipman said about intel that implicated Mac? He frowned. Not enough for him to start getting suspicious of a woman he'd just labeled a teammate, his good sense whispered back.

Go with your gut. And his gut said Mac was clean.

"Whoever was in the truck could have just picked us off in the parking lot," Mac said. "Why didn't they?"

"Too many cameras and too many people," he returned.

"Still, it's definitely time to get rid of the Vic and the tracking chip." She opened the back door for Winston and then walked around to the passenger side. "Minivan, here we come."

"That's not funny, Mac."

"It's a great cover."

He glanced at his watch. "You know, we could

pick up a flight to Denver. An hour and ten minutes, and we'd be there."

"How do you feel about excruciating pain and permanent disability?" she asked.

"It's starting to look attractive. That's how old this road trip is getting. Nothing personal, but I'm way too tall to be folded into any vehicle for long periods." He sighed. "You're sure about the ear thing?"

"Very certain. But cheer up. I'll have us in Denver in four hours."

"It's a six-and-a-half-hour drive."

"Not if I'm driving," she said.

For the first time in the last twelve hours, she smiled. It was a smile that reached her eyes and lit up her face, startling him. Gabe had forgotten about Mac's smile. It was a weapon all its own.

Yeah, she probably would get them to Denver in four hours if he let her.

He slowly shook his head. "No way. Shipman specified he wanted you alive. I'll drive."

Mac awoke with a start. Arms thrashing, she hit the back of the seat and the window at the same time.

Winston barked.

"Easy, boy," Gabe said. "She's okay."

Blinking, Mac sat up and reached into the front-passenger seat to soothe the bulldog, rubbing his ears and jowls.

She glanced around, remembering that she had crawled into the middle row of seats in the ancient, baby blue minivan that they had picked up at Toad's Clean Used Cars outside of Albuquerque.

To the west, a snow-capped peak rose into the sky. "Where are we?" she asked.

"Still on I-25. Near Colorado Springs," Gabe returned.

"What?" The realization that she'd been asleep that long left her without a response. She wiped her eyes and tried to make sense of things.

"Not a morning person, huh?" Gabe asked.

"The sun is high in the sky, so it's definitely not morning. But to answer your question, I don't know what I am anymore. I haven't slept solidly in…weeks."

"Four hours is your new personal best?"

"Four hours. I slept four hours?" She checked her watch to verify his words.

"Not to be morbid, but you were dead to the world."

"Appropriate analogy." Mac stretched, noting that she felt better than she had in weeks. Someone was trying to kill her and yet, Gabe had her back. She was no longer alone.

The realization gave her pause. Did she trust him? Apparently her head did, though the verdict was still out on her heart.

"How's your hearing?" Mac asked.

"Better. We eased into the higher altitude. That

helped." He smiled. "And I can say with certainty that I heard every single snore from the back seat."

Mac gasped, horrified. "I don't snore."

"No? Ask Winston. He'll verify."

She looked at her dog. "When did Winston get into the front?"

"We started chatting about life." Gabe shrugged. "Before I knew it, he was up here, which was probably a good thing. This has been one of the most torturously boring drives of my life."

Winston cocked his head and offered an almost apologetic whine.

"He's been sitting with you for four hours?"

"You sure ask a lot of questions. Yeah, four hours with one break. I pulled over to get bottled water from the trunk and the car stalled. So I decided it was a good time for both of us to take a stroll around the car."

"I didn't think you were a dog person."

"I've revised my opinion. Winston is different. We're buddies."

She moved her leg from the seat and grimaced. When her eyes met Gabe's, she shook her head. "I'm fine. Nothing is broken. Just the usual soreness." Which was not exactly true. She'd been knocked to the ground twice since they left Phoenix. She hurt, but there was no way she'd let Gabe feel sorry for her. He'd had his own share of trauma. Besides, they were partners now, and he wasn't her babysitter.

Gabe passed her a water. "Here. I got out an extra."

Mac yawned and took the offered bottle. "Thanks."

"Oh, and we have a new trick," he said.

"We, who?" she asked, unscrewing the lid and swigging the liquid.

"Me and my copilot here. Who do you think?" He patted Winston's head, and the animal's tail began to thump rhythmically against the seat.

Gabe raised a hand. "Give me five, Winston."

The dog lifted a paw and met Gabe's palm.

Mac released a small gasp. "How did you do that?"

"Good, right? He's a quick learner."

"You've bonded with my dog." She shook her head. "I don't get it. You seemed pretty antagonistic toward him in Phoenix."

"I was antagonistic about everything in Phoenix. Shipman pulled me from the airport boarding line on my way to a fly-fishing vacation in Ennis, Montana, for this assignment."

"What?" Mac could only stare at him. She knew how much he looked forward to his fly-fishing expeditions a few times a year.

"You'd have loved this place, Mac. Angler paradise. Streams lined with cottonwood, evergreen and willows. Then there's the lodge. Gourmet meals. Hot tubs." He gave a musing shake of his head.

"It sounds wonderful. Why didn't you mention this earlier?"

He shrugged. "There was no need."

"I'm sorry," she said. Not only had she messed with his vacation plans, but she'd also put his life in danger. Ironic, since one of the reasons she'd ended their relationship was because of the high risk their jobs entailed. Going solo through life prevented any emotional trauma, like the one that nearly destroyed her when her parents were killed.

"Don't apologize," Gabe said. "I'm over myself. Near-death experiences snap me out of self-indulgence every single time."

"If we make it out of this, I'll spring for your next trip."

"If. Again with the optimism," he scoffed and then paused. "Does that mean you'll come, too?"

"Maybe," she said. For a moment, Mac allowed her mind to wander to the fly-fishing trip they'd taken together.

It *had* been a very good trip.

When her gaze met his in the mirror, she knew he was thinking the same thing.

For a few days, she'd forgotten that her job could get someone she cared about killed.

Mac cleared her throat and pointed to a road sign for multiple traveler amenities. "How's the gas situation?"

"This baby is a gas hound, and her get-up-and-go has long gone. You should have seen me trying to pass other cars. I felt like I should put my foot outside the car to help it along."

"It's a great cover, though. Right?"

"Except for the shuddering that starts when I push it to sixty-five, the random stalling out and the door lock on the passenger side that won't open most of the time, yeah, great cover." He chuckled. "Toad saw us coming, that's for sure."

"Are you saying Toad sold us a lemon?" Mac asked with a smile.

"Yep."

A comfortable silence filled the vehicle. Then Gabe cleared his throat. "We need to check in with Shipman soon," he said.

Shipman. She'd been avoiding him since she'd escaped the shooter at the Denver rehab facility. Deep down, a slow anger simmered toward the man and the agency he represented.

They had failed her. Sure, he'd be furious that they hadn't checked in sooner, but Mac remained adamant that it was the right decision. Someone had used Gabe's trip as an opportunity to attempt to take her out. Again.

Gabe nodded at the sign that advertised gas and Golden Arches and exited the highway. He made short work of filling the tank, then drove into the parking lot of the fast-food chain next door, parking in the shade provided by a row of tall aspens.

"Looks like the perfect stop," he said. "Lots of travelers. No high ground."

No high ground meant no sniper.

One bullet and she'd be another dead CIA officer checked off someone's to-do list.

"How was the drive?" she asked. "Anything suspicious?"

"Nope."

He opened the glove box and brought out a pair of binoculars.

"Where did those come from?"

"Gas station." He got out of the minivan and did a slow one-eighty, checking the area before leaning against the van. "We're secure."

Mac eased out of the vehicle as well, biting back a groan of pain. The downside of resting was that she was stiff all over and feeling every single bruise from last night's activities. She pulled her personal phone from her messenger bag and punched in the numbers. "Here you go." She handed it to Gabe. "Shipman's secure line. On speaker."

"Sharp?" Senior Officer Shipman's booming baritone reflected relief.

"Yes, sir." Mac swallowed hard as she answered. For a moment, it was like going home. Home to that safe place before her parents died. To the time when Todd Shipman was just a family friend whose voice reminded her of all the good things life offered.

Once upon a time, before she'd been forced to erect a wall to keep herself safe.

"Denton is with you?" Shipman asked.

"I'm here, sir. You're on speaker," Gabe said.

Winston stuck his head out of the driver's-side window and barked.

"And the dog." Shipman's words were a flat commentary on his opinion of the animal. Mac let the comment pass. No one really understood her relationship with the loyal bulldog. Except maybe Gabe, she amended.

"Ah, sir," Mac began, "about Phoenix."

"I've been updated."

Mac jerked back with surprise at his words. Updated? By whom? She glanced at Gabe, whose gaze remained focused on the vehicles entering and leaving the parking lot. Maybe a little too focused.

"What's your location?" Shipman continued.

"C-Colorado," Mac stammered, her thoughts racing.

"Where in Colorado?"

She raised her palms and looked to Gabe.

"We'll be passing Larkspur next," he said.

"Renaissance festival. One hour. Joust Kitchen, inside the grounds. Brush pass."

"Yes, sir," Mac said.

"And Mackenzie," Shipman continued, "remember, a picture is worth a thousand words."

The line went dead before she could respond.

Gabe stared at the phone before handing it back to her.

"That's it?" she asked.

"One step at a time, Mac."

"Okay, sure. So what's this Joust Kitchen?"

"It's a food vendor booth."

She nodded and was silent for a moment, mulling the conversation. "Did you notice that he didn't ask any questions?" Her chest tightened, and panic bubbled up. "How did he know about Phoenix, Gabe?"

"The man is half a dozen pay grades and security clearances above us. It's his job to know things."

She paused, calculating and hating herself for where her thoughts were going. Could Shipman have sold her out? What about Gabe? And what was that cryptic comment about a picture?

Her gaze searched Gabe's, but there was nothing revealed in his hazel eyes. So if it wasn't Gabe, then Shipman somehow had tracked them. A physical ache settled in her chest, and she rubbed at the spot with the heel of her hand.

Please, Lord, not Shipman.

"You okay?" Gabe asked.

"Do you think Shipman…?" Mac paused, unable to complete the sentence.

"No, Mac. Shipman is the one person we can count on." He looked at her and released a breath. "Look, he didn't ask about Phoenix because I had already updated him. I used your burner when we stopped at that rest area outside Tucson."

"What?" She sucked in a breath. "I specifically said I didn't want to check in."

"That's you. I'm obligated to check in with Shipman. Especially when we've been compromised."

Mac's jaw tightened. The man was a total Boy Scout, and she knew that from the moment he appeared on her doorstep. She ought to be livid right now, but she couldn't fault Gabe for being Gabe and for doing his job. He had kept her alive.

So far.

Gripping her cane, she paced back and forth behind the minivan, processing.

"You're mad," he said. "I get that."

She stopped and looked at him. "If you're going to go behind my back, tell me."

"Then it wouldn't be going behind your back." He offered a grudging shrug.

Mac ignored the comment. "So why the renaissance festival?"

"Because it's close and there's no way someone will attempt a hit there. It's too crowded, and there's security walking around."

Her thoughts raced back, recalling the near-empty pier in Toronto. She could see the fog over the water, the sun rising above the shoreline. The scents of fish and sand seemed imprinted on her senses, followed by the acrid fumes of the explosion.

"Mac? You okay?"

"How crowded?" she asked, ignoring his question.

"Twelve thousand people."

"That's a lot of people," she muttered. "I don't like it."

"In and out. A simple brush pass."

"In and out was what I said about Toronto, eight weeks ago." Mac ran a hand over her face, gulping in air and willing her pulse to slow when an intense wave of anxiety threatened.

Empty pier or crowded festival. Did it really matter? It all boiled down to her and the guy holding the rifle who wanted her dead.

As if sensing her panic, Gabe pushed off the vehicle and stepped closer, his eyes locked on hers.

"Mac."

She froze, immobilized by his voice.

"Breathe. Listen to my voice and breathe."

She nodded, pursing her lips to control her respirations.

"That's it," Gabe said, his tone soothing. "We're almost to Denver. We've connected with Shipman. We're going to figure out what's going on."

Again, she nodded and began to pace once more. Then she stopped and faced Gabe.

"Shipman didn't mention Liz." She said the words that kept spinning in her head. "What about Liz?"

"He didn't say much of anything. It's only been twenty-four hours since the Agency found out about Liz. I wouldn't overthink the conversation."

Overthinking. Was that what she was doing? Overthinking and overreacting. She was trained to avoid both.

Humiliation crept over her. Mac glanced toward the front door of the Golden Arches, needing to escape. "I'm going inside to the restroom. Do you want me to pick up something for you?"

"I'll grab something when you're done."

Mac checked the contents of her messenger bag, verifying the cell and Glock remained in place before she pulled the brim low on her cap and checked the perimeter.

Winston whined and jumped into the back seat, his head popping out the window to get her attention. Mac reached into the vehicle and massaged his head. "I'll bring you back a hamburger. I promise."

The comforting aromas of salt and grease met her when she pulled open the glass door. Cane gripped tightly, Mac's steps were measured, her gaze focused as she assessed the customers on the way to the public restroom.

Any of the people in the burger place could be putting a target on her back at this moment. She picked up her pace.

When she came out of the restroom, a tour bus had pulled into the parking lot.

Talk about timing. Gabe was going to find himself behind a line of tourists. She'd go ahead and get him a burger. It was the least she could do. The guy had let her sleep for four hours.

Ahead of her, a young couple stood close, speaking quietly to each other and holding hands. Mac stared, unsure why the sweet poignancy of the scene touched her so. She remembered the early stages of her relationship with Gabe. Before she recognized that admitting that she cared meant being vulnerable, and that was a place she couldn't go.

Biting back a sigh of regret, Mac turned away from the counter with her bag of food, just as tourists began to stream in the front door. She glanced around for another exit and spotted one to the right. Cane in one hand and food sack in the other, she maneuvered with care toward the minivan.

Gabe's back was to her as he and Winston stood outside the minivan. Mac stopped on the sidewalk for a moment and watched him. Apparently he'd used the time to duck into the minivan and change into the jeans and a T-shirt he'd picked up at the box store. Relaxed, he ran a hand through his hair. The simple gesture sent her into all kinds of what-ifs. What if they'd met under different circumstances? What if they were just two people on a road trip?

Mac smiled, anticipating his reaction when he looked in his meal bag and realized she'd gotten him a kid's toy as well.

He turned slightly sideways, revealing a cell phone to his ear.

She stiffened. Where did Gabe get the phone?

Her encrypted phone and burners were in the messenger bag, nestled next to her passport and money.

Legs leaden, Mac's thoughts exploded. Who was he calling? Her stomach took a direct hit, and her head began to spin.

Was Gabe the inside source? Right in plain sight.

Her brain began a frantic scramble, searching for a response as the adrenaline of fight-or-flight kicked in.

Run? Confront him?

She had let down her guard, and it could cost her life.

At that moment, Gabe turned, and their gazes connected. He closed the phone and slipped it into his back pocket. With quick strides, he was at her side, taking the bag. "Got it."

"Where'd you get the phone?" The words escaped in a strangled effort.

"Picked it up at the last gas station. While you were sleeping." Gabe frowned. "Mac, it isn't what you think."

"No?" She stared at him, emotion rising and threatening to erupt. "Tell me what it is, Denton?" she said, her voice low and tense.

"I was securing a safe house."

"You had to do it when my back was turned?"

He released a breath and shook his head. "Are we at square one? Again?"

Was there anyone she could trust? Mac held the cane in a death grip. "Who were you talking to?"

Gabe crossed his arms and once again released a breath of frustration.

"Denton?" Mac persisted. *Please, Gabe, tell me you didn't compromise me. Tell me you didn't sell me out*, she silently pleaded.

"Avery Summers."

"Who?"

"Avery Summers. She was my fiancée." He looked around, not meeting her eyes. "Awkward, right?"

Awkward?

Yes.

And not the answer she expected, nor was the sudden spark of jealousy. Mac opened her mouth and closed it. No words came to mind as she processed the explanation of why he hadn't placed the call in front of her.

"Would you like to call Avery and verify the information?" he returned.

"Uh, no. Not necessary." Mac quickly backtracked and opened the passenger door. She took the food from him and put it on the console between the seats before sliding in.

Once Gabe was in the vehicle, he leaned back and placed his hands on the steering wheel. "It lasted all of thirty days." He looked at her and then straight ahead. "I have nothing to hide, Mac. Ask me anything."

She held up a hand. Of course Gabe had a life and relationships the last five years, but she had zero business knowing about any of it. They'd been thrust together for this mission. Confidence sharing wasn't part of the deal.

"Let's just get going," she said.

"Yeah," he said. "I'm not fighting that crowd for a burger."

Mac picked up the bag of food.

"This is for you," she said. "There's a burger in there for Winston, too."

"Thank you," he said softly.

Mac nodded, now embarrassed by her actions. "Where is this house?" she asked.

"On the outskirts of Bluebell."

"Bluebell. That's between Larkspur and Castle Rock?"

"Yeah."

"And you didn't tell Shipman."

"Thought it was safer not to."

"And your fiancée is letting you stay at her place."

"Former fiancée. And, yeah, her family opens the place to friends when they aren't there. She gave me the combo to the gate and told me where the spare key is hidden."

"Just like that?" Mac struggled to process the nature of his relationship with Avery Summers.

"Yeah, just like that. We're friends. Friends stay in touch." He raised an eyebrow. "That's how it works, Mac."

Was it? That wasn't how it worked for her. She cared too much and grieved too hard. No, she and Gabe could never be just friends.

He glanced at his watch. "Twenty minutes. We better head out to the festival. It can be bumper-to-bumper."

Gabe turned the key in the ignition, and a grinding noise sounded. The minivan worked to turn over and then gave up. "Although, if this car continues to give me grief, it could take longer." He tried once again, and the engine finally purred.

"Tell me about this house," she asked. "I need a mental layout of the place."

"The cabin is close. Maybe two miles. Sits on a couple acres. Very private."

"All good."

Gabe nodded. "A two-story alarmed dwelling with a detached garage. Forest behind the property to the south. The east side leads to more forestation and then out to I-25, and the west leads to a gully."

"Once the meet at the festival is over, you can head out," Mac said.

Gabe hit the brakes, and Mac reached out a hand to stop the food from flying everywhere.

"Whoa! What? Where did that come from? Are you dismissing me?" He practically sputtered the words, his face becoming red. Behind them, a car honked several times. Gabe pulled the minivan to the side of the road and turned to face her.

"You were supposed to get me to Denver. We're close enough." She feigned a cheerful countenance. "Mission accomplished. Frankly, the only mission of late. But it's been without much incident."

"Mission accomplished?" Disbelief echoed in his voice. "In what world are an explosion and nearly being gunned down not incidents?"

She crossed her arms, refusing to back down. "I got it from here, Gabe."

"Yeah, you got it. Right. Forget that, I'm not leaving. I don't know what's going on in that mind of yours, but I'm here for the long haul. You dismissed me once, but not this time."

Mac straightened at his words.

"Truthfully," he continued, his tone relaxing, "I'm a poor sport who's annoyed that someone got the drop on me. It's a matter of personal pride that I take down whoever blew up the rental."

"And tarnished your shiny record?" Mac regretted the words the minute she'd said them. It was a cheap shot.

His jaw tightened, as though he had to bite back a response. "We can argue about this later."

The silence between them stretched.

"Mac, look at me," Gabe finally said.

She lifted her chin.

"You have to trust somebody."

Did she?

"Yeah. You do," he responded with his irritating habit of reading her mind. "This time, you can't do it alone. Someone wants you dead. You don't know why or who to trust."

The words hit their target, exploding in her chest. What was going on? Why? Why? Why?

"You can trust me," he whispered.

Mac released a breath and pushed back the emotion threatening to give way behind the fortress she'd carefully erected. "Okay."

"But?" He paused. "There's always a *but* with you, Mac."

"Don't make me regret it, Gabe. If you do, I'll take you down in a heartbeat."

A sad smile crossed his face, almost making her want to take back her words.

"I don't doubt that for a minute," he said.

FIVE

"Huzzah."

"Excuse me?" Mac looked up from the map on her phone and shot Gabe a questioning glance.

"Huzzah. It's Russian." Gabe pointed at a sign for the Colorado Renaissance Festival that came into view.

"Technically not," Mac said. "It says here on the festival website that it's a term of joy and awesome delight."

"Always literal, Mac." He gave a headshake that said he didn't quite get her. "Have you ever been to a renaissance festival?"

"Um, no. I never saw the point."

"The point is it's a festival. Knights and queens and kings. All things medieval fun."

Unimpressed, she continued to scroll through the information on her phone. "According to the online schedule, we're too late for both the royal procession and the knighting ceremony."

"We'll come back," Gabe said.

"I was joking." There wouldn't be any coming back. They'd be fortunate to be alive the next time the royal procession appeared. And if they were, well, she and Gabe lived in two different worlds. They'd smile and go their separate ways once the dust cleared.

"Did you find a map of the festival grounds?" he asked, glancing over at her phone.

"Yes. The place is huge. Sixty acres. Shipman chose a location close to the entrance. We enter and turn left. The Joust Kitchen is near an emergency exit."

Mac relaxed a bit at the information. Even if things went south, they were close enough to an exit to ensure a rapid retreat. At this point, she was grasping for anything that would keep today's meet from turning into a repeat of Toronto, and an emergency exit would do fine.

"Turkey legs," Gabe said.

"What?" She blinked and looked up, processing his words. "You had a burger twenty minutes ago."

"We're being targeted by someone who wants us dead. If my last meal is a turkey leg, so be it."

"Your rationale is not rational."

"According to you," he returned with a grin.

Mac stared at his profile for a moment. She'd missed verbally sparring with Gabe. There were times like now when she got a snapshot of what it would be like to be a woman without fear as her constant companion. A woman who could consider the possibility of a relationship...with a guy just like Gabe Denton.

The clicking sound of the turning indicator echoed through the minivan before Gabe directed the vehicle down the road to the festival parking.

"The parking area is packed," Mac observed.

"It's Saturday, and it's the Colorado Renaissance Festival," Gabe said. "Looks like the traffic is moving along, though."

"That's because it closes in two hours." She tapped her fingers on the messenger bag on her lap. "And we now have eleven minutes to get to the Joust Kitchen."

"Relax, Mac. We got this."

Gabe followed a small line of cars into a parking lot and then complied with the hand directions of an attendant with an orange vest, who pointed them to an open space at the end of a row.

Mac's gaze moved to a cluster of people in medieval costumes at the ticket building to the left of a brick sixteenth-century Tudor-village facade. "It appears we aren't dressed for the occasion," she said.

"Cosplay. I'm not into ankle-banded breeches and blouses myself." He reached for his blazer and holster in the back seat. "Makes it difficult to hide a SIG Sauer."

"I have no idea what banded breeches are," Mac said. She rolled up her pant leg and tucked her weapon into an ankle holster, then put her phone in her back pocket. In a perfect world, she wouldn't have to use the weapon. There were far too many people here to make that choice a good option.

After leashing Winston, she picked up her cane from the back seat and got out of the vehicle. Despite the cane, she moved awkwardly as the gravel beneath her feet shifted.

"Why don't I take Winston?" Gabe asked.

"Are dogs even allowed in the festival grounds?"

"Special Agent Winston is."

She smiled at his humor, grateful for the offer. It was humiliating that a simple task like walking across gravel required acute concentration. Would she ever again be fit for her job? Maybe it was time for a change, her mind whispered. Mac pushed aside the thought and increased her pace.

By the time she caught up with Gabe and Winston, they were at the front of the ticket line at Ye Olde Box Office.

A woman wearing a puffy-sleeved peasant blouse and a laced corset offered Gabe an inviting smile. The name tag that she wore identified her as Gwendolyn. "Welcome, milord and lady." She eyed Winston. "Would your beast be a service dog?"

Gabe pulled out his identification and quietly slid it across the counter. Mac did the same. "Right now, he's in service to his country. Winston is assisting a federal agent."

The woman's eyes rounded. "Shall I summon the boss?"

"Not necessary." He leaned close and lowered his voice. "I trust you can handle confidential information, Gwendolyn?"

"Yes, milord."

"Two tickets, then. Three, if Winston needs one." He smiled. "And, by the way, nice outfit."

She grinned. "I thank ye."

Once again, Mac admired his easy people skills as the woman handed over the tickets without further objection.

"I don't see any security," Mac said.

"Over there," Gabe said. "LEO at your one o'clock."

Mac turned casually and spotted both male and female local law enforcement carefully monitoring the stream of people walking in and out of the festival's Tudor fortress walls.

Head down, Mac followed Gabe and moved beneath the arched entrance into the crowded realm of the renaissance festival. Around them, costumed revelers walked the village-like streets, as did couples and families with strollers. Mac found herself both intrigued and confused by the costumes.

To her right, a medieval piper played while villagers danced to the music.

"This way." Gabe pointed toward a rustic sign that listed the Joust Kitchen. "Left at the fountain."

"I'm right behind you," Mac said while struggling to assess the many people she passed. Festival shop windows offered capes and hats and various medieval attire. It would be easy for someone targeting them to slip into a disguise quickly. It was already difficult to tell the festival staff from the costumed attendees, which made identifying a threat nearly impossible.

She'd almost caught up with Gabe when a barrel-chested vendor stepped into her path. The man's large, thick hands held a tall pole with bags of cinnamon-roasted almonds dangling from pegs. Dressed in a kilt and sleeveless blouse that displayed impressive tattoos, he loomed over her, blocking the summer sky.

"Almonds, milady?" he boomed.

Before Mac could answer, Gabe was at her side, taking her hand and tucking her arm beneath his. "Come on, honey. The turkey legs are this way."

"Thank you," she breathed as Gabe led her away. "That guy was a little scary."

"Yeah, but there was no way he was concealing a weapon."

"You're right. But he could have broken me in two with his bare hands."

Farther down the path, the Joust Kitchen appeared. A two-story building had been constructed to resemble a portion of a medieval village, with storefronts lined up next to each other like houses, each hosting a food vendor.

A bold sign advised that the shops accepted Her Lady Visa and Master Card.

"How about if you watch the front and Winston and I circle the building?" Gabe said. When he released her hand, Mac couldn't help but recall the easy times in the past when holding hands wasn't part of an undercover assignment. She'd taken Gabe's affection for granted five years ago.

As Gabe and Winston left her line of sight, Mac stepped into the shadows and found a position where she could observe everyone walking by. Her back was to an oak tree, whose branches partially concealed her.

When they reappeared on the other side of the building minutes later, Gabe stopped a few feet in front of her and knelt down, pretending to adjust Winston's harness and leash as he assessed the foot traffic. Typically, the Agency sent unknown operatives to a brush pass.

"Do you recognize anyone who could be an operative?" Mac asked under her breath.

"Blake Calder."

She tensed. "Blake Calder? Who is he?"

"Shipman's right-hand guy. He's up there on the food chain but he's new to the Denver office. No one following us would recognize the guy."

"The name doesn't ring a bell."

"No reason it would. He showed up six weeks or so ago." Gabe nodded in front of them. "That's him. Stuffed shirt studying the chalkboard menu. The guy with the backpack."

Mac spotted him. Tall and starched with close-cropped, nondescript brown hair. Any other time and she'd have laughed at the irony. He reminded her of Gabe when he'd shown up at her door in Phoenix last night. One-hundred-percent government-issue.

"Do you trust him?" she asked.

"Shipman does. I'm guessing that's why he sent a desk jockey into the field. That and the fact that he's unknown."

"That's not what I asked."

"I don't have enough information to make that determination."

Gabe stepped up to the food building, while Mac moved to his right and got in a slow-moving beverage line.

"Looks good, doesn't it?" Calder said to Gabe as the officer continued to peruse the vendor's offerings.

"Yeah," Gabe returned. "I'm thinking about the turkey drumstick, though I've got to admit, the Earl of Bratwurst sounds good."

With a discreet nod to Mac, Calder stepped into the line next to hers, directly to her left. He casually placed the backpack on the ground next to her feet and then reached in his pocket, pulling out a wallet.

Mac took the moment to scoop up the backpack and ease out of line.

Minutes later, Calder left the counter with a plate of food in his hand. He met Mac's gaze head-on before turning away and disappearing into the crowd.

She didn't know the guy, yet there was something familiar about him. What?

"You sure you don't want a turkey leg?" Gabe asked. He stood a few feet from her with Winston.

"I know him from somewhere." Mac continued to watch the crowd that had swallowed the CIA officer.

"Calder?"

"Yes." She nodded and shivered. "And it's going to bug me until I figure it out."

"It will come to you eventually." Gabe studied the turkey leg, resting in a shallow red-and-white-checked bowl, then tore into it with his usual enthusiasm.

"*Eventually* isn't good enough. There's just so much muddled in my head. Toronto and then the Denver shooting. I was taking a lot of pain meds in rehab, too." She adjusted the backpack and looked at Gabe. "How do you know him?"

"Met him briefly yesterday, when I arrived in Denver. Most of the staff had gone home. I was serious. He really is Shipman's new right-hand guy."

Mac was silent as she tried to put together a few more pieces of the puzzle that comprised her life right now.

"Will you please hurry up and eat that so we can get out of here?" she asked Gabe.

"Almost done," Gabe said. "Something looks suspicious to you?"

"The whole world looks suspicious to me. Case in point—there's a masked man in a velvet cape eating a pork chop on a stick behind you. Then there's the guy with the chain-mail suit and a sword at my twelve o'clock. This place is a security nightmare."

"You might be overreacting," Gabe said.

She nodded toward a woman with a dragon on her shoulder. "The skirt of that dress could hide a rocket-propelled grenade."

"And you've got a vivid imagination." He tossed the remains of the turkey leg into a trash receptacle and wiped his hands. "Let's go."

As they stepped through the arch and outside the festival entrance, Mac froze, her eyes on the parking lot. "Black pickup in the front row there."

"Yeah, and there's probably fifty black trucks in this lot."

Mac rubbed her arms. It was at least ninety degrees out, yet she was suddenly very cold. "Gabe, I have a bad feeling."

"We've been here for...what? Thirty minutes? The only way anyone could have found us is if they knew we'd be here."

"What about that one? Twelve o'clock. Ford F-150 with a raptor grille. Just like our would-be carjackers described." His gaze followed hers to the black pickup, which was slowly moving through the parking area.

Gabe tensed as he assessed the vehicle, then pulled Winston back into the shadows with him. "You're right. Good call."

"Let's split up," Mac said. "You go left, and I'll go right. Meet you at the minivan."

"That's a terrible idea. You stay put, over there by the ticket building, out of sight. I'll get the minivan and pick you up."

She opened her mouth to mount a rebuttal, but Gabe's expression caused her to rethink arguing the point.

"Mac, please. Could we do it my way, this time?"

"Why your way?"

"Because even though you're the prickliest woman I've ever known, once again you're starting to grow on me. I'd like to figure out why. And I can't do that if you're dead."

"I…" Mac sputtered, confused by his response. "Okay, fine, but we're going to have to discuss the terms of this so-called partnership. Soon."

"Nicely done," Gabe said once they were clear of the festival grounds. He shrugged out of his blazer and tossed it in the back seat before his gaze went to the rearview mirror again. "We're clear. So far."

"How did you get rid of the pickup truck?"

"Didn't get rid of him, but definitely slowed him

down. I told the parking attendant that the driver had overindulged, appeared impaired. I might have suggested that he had illegal substances in the vehicle as well. The attendant radioed law enforcement and they surrounded the truck."

"Nicely done," Mac murmured.

He expected more commentary, but she turned her attention out the window. Still, he didn't regret his outburst outside the festival entrance. Keeping Mac alive was the goal here, and if he had to reveal a few personal cards along the way, so be it.

"Where's your friend's house?" she asked minutes later.

"We've already passed the turnoff for Bluebell. I'll circle back down a few of these rural roads until I'm sure we aren't being followed." He handed her his phone. "I have the directions pulled up."

They drove in silence until Gabe turned back onto a less remote thoroughfare.

Mac flipped down the mirror. "We've got a tail." She released a breath.

"The pickup truck?"

"No. Two cars back. Check out the yellow commercial moving truck. Small, maybe a ten-footer."

"This is getting old," Gabe said.

"Tell me about it." She assessed the map on his phone. "There's a left turn coming up, one quarter of a mile. It looks like it goes straight through."

"Okay, hang on."

Gabe gripped the steering wheel, braked and then made a hard left without signaling. He immediately accelerated, pulling them through the turn. Behind him, horns blared.

"He's still coming. Fast," Mac said.

"Can you see plates?" Gabe asked. "Maybe we can find out who rented the vehicle."

"Front license plate is obscured with mud."

"Can you see who's in there?"

"Male. Caucasian. Looks tall. He has a ball cap and sunglasses…" Mac paused and her face paled.

"What is it, Mac?"

"That guy could be the shooter."

"From Toronto?"

She swallowed. "Yes."

Gabe's eyes moved from the two-lane road to the rearview mirror and back again, as he prayed for a diversion.

"Train crossing straight ahead, Gabe."

He sucked in a breath as the vehicle in front of the minivan made it across the tracks before the white-and-red-checkered arms lowered, cutting them off from safety on the other side. The red lights on the arms flashed a silent warning.

"Can you hear a train approaching?" Gabe debated pulling a U-turn in the limited space and discarded the idea. If the guy had a weapon he'd easily take them out.

Mac rolled down her window and nodded. "I don't see it yet, but I can hear it."

Behind them, the moving truck revved the engine. The driver had pulled down the visor, and Gabe was unable to get a clear view of the man behind the wheel.

Mac unfastened her seat belt and crawled into the back seat, taking the messenger bag and the backpack with her.

"What are you doing?" Gabe asked.

"I'm protecting Winston, in case that guy has a weapon." She grabbed Gabe's blazer and cocooned the dog in the material.

Gabe studied the train tracks and shot the vehicle behind them a quick glance while he weighed the options. In a heartbeat, he decided. Their only chance was on the other side of the barrier arms.

"Brace yourself, Mac. I'm going to accelerate and try to get past those barrier arms."

"You mean right through them?"

"Exactly." As he said the words, Gabe floored the vehicle, gripping the steering wheel tightly when his body propelled backward, then forward, and the minivan made contact with the arms. The crunching sound of impact filled the air.

Then the minivan shuddered and came to a stop. Like spiderwebs, cracks in the windshield appeared where the arms made contact. Gabe turned to look out the rear window, where the crossing arms hung limp and defeated.

"What's happening, Gabe?" Mac called.

"Stalled." As he said the word, the rear window

of the minivan exploded, sending glass into the vehicle. Gabe jerked with surprise, then quickly unlatched his seat belt. He slid down in the seat and pulled his weapon from its holster.

"Stay down, Mac," Gabe yelled. "He's up close and personal with a rifle."

"Trust me. I'm down."

Once again, Gabe tried the engine, while silently pleading. The result was a grinding noise. He hit the steering wheel with his hand in frustration.

"We have to get out," Mac said.

Gabe angled himself to look into the back seat, where he saw Mac reach for her ready bag and pull out another magazine for her Glock.

"Gabe! Are you listening to me? We can't just sit here on the tracks," Mac said. "This is not how I planned to die."

He agreed with the sentiment. Anger at the situation threatened, but he tamped it down, letting his training take over.

"If we make a run for it, we do it together." As Gabe spoke, the truck behind them edged closer and the driver's-side door opened.

Gabe opened his door, too. "Stay down, Mac." He turned in his seat and held his weapon steady, hand resting on the headrest as he prepared to return fire.

"Can you see the train?" she asked.

He shot a quick glance over his shoulder. "Not

yet. The track bends around a corner. But I can hear it loud and clear."

"We need to get across the tracks." Mac's fingers worked furiously on the phone screen. "And we have about three minutes to do it before the BNSF coal train arrives."

"Lord, I could use a little help here," he muttered.

"I agree with that prayer," Mac said.

Another shot rang out, this time shattering the minivan's driver's-side mirror. Gabe jumped away from the flying glass.

"No matter what, I want you to keep your head down," he said. "I'll cover you. When I give the signal, you and Winston head to those trees on the right."

"What about you?"

"I'll be fine." He could only pray that was the truth. On a whim, he turned in his seat and tried the ignition once more.

The engine turned over.

"Thank You," he murmured on a shaky breath.

Relief was short-lived as the piercing sound of the approaching locomotive got louder and louder.

Gabe put the vehicle into Drive and floored it. His door closed by itself with the forward momentum.

The minivan flew over the tracks, kicking up a cloud of dirt and gravel when they landed on the other side. He resisted the urge to look back, and instead kept going, all the while praying under his breath. Seconds later, the train flashed past, the force and speed making the vehicle's windows rattle.

"I think I'm going to be sick," Mac said.

"You want me to pull over? Now?"

"No. No. Keep going."

Gabe accelerated, though his hands were shaking and his heart galloping. He glanced in the back seat, where Mac was lying on the floor. It was one thing to have his life on the line, but Mac and Winston? He wasn't used to being responsible for anyone else.

"Mac, are you okay? Where's Winston?"

"Under the seat. He's shaken but fine."

Gabe grimaced when she looked up and he noted the blood on her face. He was supposed to keep her safe.

"What's that look for?"

"There's blood on your forehead."

Mac put a hand to her head, gingerly touched the area and shrugged. "Some flying glass. I'm fine." She reached into the front seat and put a hand on his arm. "Nice job, partner."

Partner? For a moment he savored the word that he never thought he'd hear from Mac. Then reality hit.

Gabe released a breath and pointed heavenward. "I've got a feeling it was our other partner who saved us."

SIX

"Hang on, Mac. The house is alarmed."

At Gabe's voice, Mac stepped back from the open doorway of the home he'd brought them to. She eased down onto the wrought-iron bench beneath the covered portico and said a small prayer for patience.

Praying. That was Gabe's influence.

Winston whined and shoved his snout into her arm. The bulldog was no doubt confused. It was nearly 6:00 p.m., yet it seemed like midnight.

"I know, boy. I know." She rubbed the dog's ears and sleek brown-and-white coat before she buried her face into his neck for a moment. Oh, how she loved this animal. He'd provided unconditional love from day one, accepting her and all her antisocial quirks. Right now, while she was still trembling from the near collision with the coal train, a hug from Winston made all the difference.

Soon they both could relax and forget for a little

while that nearly every moment of the last twenty hours had been disastrous. The last hour, particularly nightmarish. Even the unflappable, optimistic Gabe seemed subdued.

A beep sounded, indicating that Gabe had disarmed the system. A moment later he poked his head out the door. "Let me check the place."

"We can sweep it faster together," she said.

"I've got this." His tone was resolute.

"Fine."

It was only minutes before he returned to the front door. "It's clear."

Mac looked up and adjusted the backpack and her messenger bag. Exhaustion now paired with pain as she struggled to stand.

"Let me help," Gabe said.

When he offered his arm for her to lean on, she hesitated and then nodded. "Thanks." There was no point in being a martyr.

Gabe handed her the cane once she was standing, and she and Winston followed him into the house. Mac stepped into a huge living area and stopped.

"Gabe, this isn't even close to being a cabin."

"Did I say 'cabin'?"

"Yes. You did." She'd picked up enough copies of *Architectural Digest* in physician waiting rooms to appreciate that this house would fit right in an issue titled *Ski Lodge Decor*. While it hinted at rustic, the home was high-end interior design, from the massive stone fireplace to the vaulted, planked wood ceiling and walls.

"This place is amazing." Her gaze went to the tall windows and the double doors leading to a veranda, and she shook her head.

"You're right." Gabe addressed her unspoken thoughts. "Those windows are a concern. I think the blinds are electric." He moved to the wall. "Yeah, here's the controls, but there should be a remote around here, too."

"The woods," Mac said. She stared out the window at the dense grouping of conifers. "A hundred yards away?"

Gabe nodded, his gaze intense, as he, too, stared out at the trees.

"Hmm." A sniper in a deer blind could make the shot with even a mediocre skill level. That information would keep them awake tonight.

"What about the other windows?" she asked.

"The kitchen has a floor-to-ceiling window as well, also facing the trees. The other windows are reinforced and much smaller."

Mac slowly strolled around the room, careful not to slip on the shiny oak floors. "Not a cabin, Gabe. This place is serious real estate."

"Yeah, it's nice," he said.

Nice? She turned around to face him, unable to resist asking a few questions. "How did you and Anne-Marie…"

"Avery."

"Avery," Mac murmured. "So how did you two meet?"

The woman was likely a physician to underserved populations while simultaneously researching a cure for a rare disease that would put her in the running for a Nobel Prize.

Not that it was any of her business or anything.

Gabe chuckled and watched her for a moment. He'd always had the unnerving ability to make her feel as though he knew exactly what she was thinking.

"Avery is a model. We met at a fundraising event my father invited me to on Capitol Hill."

Mac blinked. A model. She resisted the urge to look down at her rumpled jeans and T-shirt.

"So, um, I guess that explains that picture on the wall." She pointed to a framed photo of several men she didn't recognize with the current President of the United States.

"Um, yeah. Her father is big in political circles."

That explained a lot, too. Yes, she could see how Gabe's father would have approved of a merger with this family. The fact left a sour taste in her mouth.

"Politics," she said. "Nice."

"Your father was an ambassador," he countered.

"To a country that no longer exists."

Mac frowned, suddenly annoyed at herself for her catty and, yes, jealous behavior. Though that failed to stop her mouth from running. "Don't try to put me in the same lane as your fiancée. She's moneyed. Her family is powerful."

"Ex-fiancée."

At Gabe's short response, she paused, horrified at her behavior, and backpedaled. "I just wondered what you'd been doing for the last five years. Now I know. Discussion closed."

"Not hardly," he murmured.

Mac pressed on, hoping to change the subject quickly. She ran a hand over the back of a buttery soft oversize leather lodge sofa and glanced around. "I'm a little nervous about staying here. What if I spill something?"

"They have a service that comes in to clean the place in between guests." He nodded toward the door. "I'll get everything out of the minivan. Including the first-aid kit. Your head needs attention."

"My head is fine, but thank you." She walked from the living area to an open-design kitchen and placed the backpack on the farmhouse table.

Minutes later, Gabe returned carrying the duffle bags and supplies. Winston followed with his food dish between his teeth, his nails clicking on the oak floor.

"Mind if I feed Winston?" he asked.

"That would be great, although I will warn you that if he identifies you as the source of food, you'll be the one he wakes up at six a.m."

Gabe chuckled. "I can deal with that."

Mac pulled a slim laptop and a thumb drive on a key chain from the backpack and put them on the table. She carefully inspected the pockets and seams of the pack for a tracking device, but found nothing.

Behind her, the sound of kibble being poured into a bowl, followed by running water, indicated Winston had been fed.

Mac powered up the laptop and examined the drives. It appeared to be clean. Once she had inserted and opened the thumb drive, she frowned at the contents.

"What's the matter?" Gabe asked.

"Well, look. I think it's entirely dog photos."

"I can see that." He stood behind her again, and she could feel his warm breath on her neck and shivered.

She pushed out a chair for him with her foot. "Have a seat."

Gabe turned the slatted chair around, then straddled it.

One by one, Mac went through the pictures, which consisted of images of the Shipman family's Labrador retrievers. One golden and one chocolate. "Why would he send me photos of Milo and Chloe?" she asked.

"They are beautiful dogs, but I'm guessing there's more here."

Mac continued to review the file until she came

to the last image. It had discolored edges and a line through the center, as if folded at one time.

She nearly gasped aloud. The photo was of the Sharp family and the Shipman family sitting around a table. Thanksgiving. She remembered this photo. Shipman's children, Megan and Lance, were a decade younger than Mac, but they were like one big family. She enlarged the screen and stared at the T-shirt she wore. It was a high-school track-team shirt, with her school and the year emblazoned on the front. This photo had been taken six months before her parents died.

Such a joyous moment in time. It would be only months until their world would be turned upside down.

"You okay, Mac?" Gabe put a comforting hand on her shoulder.

She nodded. "Yes. Yes. All good."

"Where was that picture taken?"

"My house. My parents' house. They owned a place in Georgetown." Mac placed her fingers against her mouth, and for a moment was transported back. For the first time in a long time, the memories didn't trigger anxiety. Maybe that meant she was healing.

"Mac?" Gabe's gentle query pulled her from her thoughts.

"I'm good." She turned to him. "Why would he send me this picture?" And then it hit her. "That's it. Remember what he said?"

"What?"

"A picture is worth a thousand words. This is steganography. Microdots and cipher codes. It's a hobby of Shipman's. He's a real World War II cipher buff." Mac magnified the picture until she could see the tiny dots. Then she enlarged each dot.

"I see the letters. How did you know that?"

"Shipman taught me. It was a distraction after my parents died. He and I would send steganographic files back and forth. A sort of treasure hunt." She smiled. "We haven't done that in…over sixteen years." She closed her eyes for a moment and again smiled. When she was in college, on the anniversary of her parents' death, he'd sent her on a steganography treasure hunt. One that took hours and kept her from dwelling on sad memories of the day, and subsequent weeks, when her life changed forever.

Todd Shipman was a good man.

"You were pretty close with the Shipmans. I mean, you lived with them your senior year of high school and all."

"I was closest to Todd. Probably because he was so much like my father. They'd been best friends since college." Sometimes she forgot what he lost on the day of the embassy attack. The grief wasn't hers alone.

"Long time." He cocked his head. "Do you still remember the encryption key you two used?"

"Yes. It was a basic symmetric encryption."

"Basic encryption?"

"Basic with a twist that Shipman added." Mac smiled as she recalled when he first taught her the code. The world had moved to being high-tech, but sometimes the basics and old-school ciphers were all that was needed.

"Okay," Gabe said.

"He's very clever. If the laptop was intercepted it's unlikely anyone would catch this, or break the code quickly." She glanced around. "Do you suppose there's paper and a pencil in a drawer somewhere?"

"Yeah, sure." He stood and walked out of the room, returning with a pencil and notebook a few minutes later.

"Thanks." She began to scribble, transcribing the cipher, excitement building as she worked. The letters formed words and then sentences. When she'd finished, Mac gasped.

"What is it?"

"He's telling me that a bank account was opened in a Denver bank using my social security number and personal data." Mac shook her head in disbelief.

Gabe remained silent, obviously deep in thought.

"Five hundred thousand dollars was deposited into the account by wire transfer from an offshore account." She leaned back in her seat, working to take it all in.

"How would someone get that information?" Gabe asked.

"Information? Where would someone get that kind of money?" Then she paused before answering her own question. "They'd get it from the Toronto bank job. And the account was opened within five days of that mission going south."

"Yep. Launder the money through an offshore account and then send it out into the world."

"Five hundred thousand dollars would easily raise a red flag. And if not? A tip-off to the right agencies, and before you know it, I'm being investigated for a possible connection to the robbery." She released a breath and snapped her fingers. "Putting me in the crosshairs of Homeland Security."

With this information, things had gone from bad to worse, though the last thing she should do was let her emotions get in the way. It was still a mission and she was trained to handle even the most challenging assignments.

"Whoever masterminded this has a good understanding of how the system works," Gabe said. "And they're high enough on the food chain to be able to access personnel information at the Agency, is my guess."

Mac tapped her pencil on the table. "Shipman is buying me time to figure things out for myself before he has no choice but to order me to come in."

Anxiety began to rise as she stared at the paper.

"I don't know where to start." She looked at him. "You said there was a security breach at the Denver office."

Gabe ran a hand over his face. "Yeah, and there's something else. When I spoke to Shipman last night, he mentioned that the Agency had received intel. Intel that, if true, could implicate you in the Toronto bank job. Now I know this is what he was talking about."

"Why didn't you tell me?" She stared, stunned by the admission.

"Shipman didn't give me details and I didn't believe it was true. There was no point adding to your stress then."

"You should have told me."

"I'm sorry, but I never for a minute even considered it to be legit intel. It hadn't been verified when he told me."

"Looks like it's been verified, all right," Mac murmured. She was silent for a moment, processing the new information. "I appreciate your belief in me," she said. "I don't deserve that after the way I treated you."

Gabe put his hand over hers. The gesture surprised her, yet she didn't move away, instead savoring his touch before looking up to meet his gaze.

"Mac, you're dedicated to your job and your country. To a fault. It wasn't until my mother's death that I began to understand where your headspace was five years ago. I get it now."

"You're a very generous man." She sighed, confused and overwhelmed by everything.

Step by step, someone was trying to silence her. If they couldn't kill her, they'd burn her career with the Agency. This new information moved the stakes to a whole new level, and she couldn't allow Gabe to get in the middle of a situation that could ruin his own career.

"You should leave," she said as she slipped her hand from beneath his.

"That's the second time you've said that. Is there a particular reason why you're continually trying to get rid of me?"

"You have a lot more to lose than I do. A promising young man. Isn't that how Shipman refers to you? I heard he's recommended you for a position at The Farm."

"How did you hear that?" He shook his head. "Doesn't matter. I'm not leaving. If I were going to leave, it would have been in Phoenix."

"There's nothing you can do. It won't take long before the Agency directs me to come in. When I don't, I'll be considered rogue." Mac cringed at her own words. She'd spent her life up until now serving her country and that service was about to become null and void.

"We need help," Gabe said.

"We? There is no *we*."

"I thought you trusted me. Agreed we're partners."

"Partners." She said the word slowly, recalling their near-death escape on the train tracks. Her thoughts immediately went to her Agency partner, Liz Morrow. What sort of unspeakable situation was she in right now?

"What are you thinking?" he asked.

"Shipman didn't mention Liz," Mac said.

"He gave you what you need to know to plan your next strategy. We have to trust that he's handling the Morrow situation. That's his job, and Shipman is very good at what he does."

"You're right." Mac nodded, though being right did little to assuage the guilt that haunted her about Liz's situation.

"We're running out of time here. We can't count on the Agency to help us. I'm calling my brother."

"Ben? I thought he was in the army. Army ranger training officer, wasn't it?" She'd met the older Denton brother a time or two. He was a good guy, like Gabe.

"Good memory," Gabe said. "Ben moved over to intelligence a few years ago and then got out."

"Out? After all those tours he's logged, I can't believe your brother is a civilian."

"Decided he wanted to do something in the private sector."

"Like what?"

"Security. Denton Security and Investigations is the official name."

She mulled over that information. Ben had connections in the intelligence world. Maybe he could even help them find answers about Liz.

"He's trying to get me to join him."

"What?" Mac looked up. "I'm sorry, what did you say?"

"I said that he's trying to get me to join his company."

She nodded. "And you turned him down. Why?"

Gabe raised an eyebrow in question. "How do you know I turned him down?"

Mac was silent, searching for a response. "I know you." She knew he wasn't ready to buck his father and clearly he wasn't going to discuss it, either.

He stared at her for a moment.

"Okay, yeah, I turned him down. Maybe someday."

"Someday is an illusion, Gabe."

He released a breath. "Man, next to you, I'm unicorns and rainbows."

"I'm just saying you should do what you really want. Not what someone else wants you to do."

"What about you, Mac? What do you want?"

She glanced away and fiddled with the pencil and notebook on the table. It hadn't escaped her that the advice she so easily doled out applied to her as well. Would she have the guts to do what she'd encouraged him to do?

"We aren't talking about me," she finally said.

Gabe shook his head, clearly communicating

that her response was as silly as it sounded. "Why not? Don't you deserve happiness?"

Happiness. Mac nearly scoffed aloud. *Happiness* had never been a word in her vocabulary. She didn't deserve it, or expect it.

"So where is Ben living?"

"Good dodge." He picked up his phone. "He's headquartered in DC, but works all over the country. I'm going to text him."

"And I'm going to look for coffee." Her stomach rumbled as she stood. A glance at the clock on the stove reminded her that she hadn't eaten since Albuquerque.

She opened the cupboard above a fancy chrome-and-black espresso machine and found a bag of overpriced coffee beans. Mac unsealed the bag and sniffed. Stale. The date was six months ago. Ski season. Probably the last time anyone had visited the house.

At the kitchen door, Winston barked and thumped his tail on the floor.

"What is it, boy?" Mac went to the door in time to see a squirrel dancing around a tree, teasing the bulldog.

Her gaze went to the expansive yard that surrounded the house. The forest provided a silent barricade during the day. But, already, the sun was lower in the sky. Dusk would be upon them in a few hours, and then, they wouldn't be able to see what was hiding in the trees.

"Ben will be here late tonight," Gabe said. "Around midnight or so."

"That fast?"

"He's dating a commercial pilot, and she got him a standby seat on a flight to Denver."

"What did you tell him?"

"As little as possible. His phone wasn't secure. I said that I was in Denver with you, and it was urgent and classified."

"That's it? That's all you said, and he's on the next plane to Denver?"

Gabe shot her a confused look. "Well, yeah. He's my brother."

"Wow, that's loyalty. You're fortunate." As a single child, she didn't have the luxury of a sibling for support, and she found herself envious.

"Yeah, I am." He stood. "Not to change the subject, but my stomach says that it's time to eat."

"Mine, too. Is there anything to work with here?"

"They keep it stocked." Gabe pulled open the fridge, and then he turned to look at her with a sheepish expression. "Is it wrong that I'm craving pizza?"

Mac nearly laughed. "I thought you were fixated on Thai."

"That was until we passed that mom-and-pop pizzeria. We can do Thai on Sunday."

"Ugh." Mac slumped. "Is it really only Saturday night? We can't go into the field office to meet with Shipman until Monday," she said. "I can't sit around doing nothing until then."

Gabe's eyes rounded. "Going to the field office was the old plan. Shipman was warning us to stay away. If we go in, you could be arrested and I'll be charged with obstruction of justice."

She nearly gasped aloud as the truth hit home. "You're right. What are we going to do?"

"We'll head out early and monitor who goes into the field office. I want to ID the tech who gave me that security card and lanyard."

He closed the refrigerator. "Do you have a burner phone that we haven't used yet?"

"I do." She dug in the messenger bag and pulled it out.

"Cash?"

Mac nodded. "Where are you going with this?"

"I'll place a pizza order with the burner."

She perked up. "Okay. But absolutely no pineapple, Gabe."

He laughed. "You remembered."

"Who could forget?" Mac shuddered. "I'm willing to compromise here. Just no pineapple."

"Deal."

"I don't suppose we could do a grocery-store run. I've been dreaming of drinking a cup of coffee without being worried that I was going to die."

"There's got to be coffee in the cupboard to feed that beast of a machine on the counter."

"I'm particular about my coffee. The beans in the cupboard are past their prime."

Gabe shook his head. "A grocery store is pushing it. Bluebell is a small town. A baby blue minivan with the rear window shot out is not going to go unnoticed. The driver's-side mirror? Useless as well. That'll get us pulled over in a heartbeat."

"You're right."

"I'll text Ben and tell him to bring coffee."

"Really?"

"Coffee is important to you. I get that."

Yes, he did, and Mac melted a little at his words.

He smiled and went over to play with Winston, leaving Mac with the dawning realization that as much as she reminded herself that Gabe Denton was her past, her heart obviously hadn't read the memo.

Winston jumped up and gave a frenzied bark when the buzzer from the door intercom sounded. Gabe followed the animal to the front door. "Sit," he commanded the bulldog.

He glanced at his watch. One a.m. His brother had made good time from the airport.

"Gabe?" Mac called from the kitchen, her voice tense.

"Relax. It's Ben. He just texted me." Gabe stepped out to the front yard, where a trail of solar walkway lights lit up the darkness of the summer night. A warm breeze said hello, reminding him that for most of the residents of the peaceful town of Bluebell, Colorado, this was just a nice July evening.

Ben stood outside with a duffle bag and small suitcase. Gabe had always admired his brother's effortless polished look, and tonight was no different. His dark hair remained military-short, and he wore black trousers and a crisp white shirt with nary a wrinkle. He tried to emulate his big brother, but one look in the mirror always told him, once a nerd, always a nerd.

"Gabriel. Long time no see," Ben called.

Gabe grinned. Ben was the only person who got away with calling him by the full name their mother had chosen for him. "Gabriel, God, is my strength," she often said.

A surge of relief flooded Gabe, his spirit lifted at the sight of his big brother, and he let him know with a man-hug and grin. "Thanks for coming."

"Thanks for trusting me to help."

"How'd you get a rental this time of night?" Gabe asked.

"I pulled in a favor."

"Of course you did." They walked into the house, where Mac was waiting with Winston. She'd showered and changed clothes, and he found himself proud of how she stood tall and welcoming, though she had to be exhausted and hurting.

She reached out awkwardly to hug Ben and then ended up shaking his hand.

"Good to see you again, Mackenzie." Ben reached in his duffle and pulled out a small paper bag. "You requested coffee."

Gabe could smell the rich aroma of fresh beans from where he stood.

"Oh, Ben. Thank you."

"My pleasure." He looked at Winston. "Who's this fella?"

"This is Winston," Mac said.

"Churchill?"

"Yes."

Ben nodded. "Never, never, never give up." He offered the quote with a deep voice, his eyebrows knitted together as though imitating the British leader.

"Yes." Mac's face lit up at the words. "You sound just like him."

Gabe frowned at the exchange. He didn't remember them getting along so well.

"So what's the story with the clunker out there?" Ben asked. He looked at Gabe, and stepped closer, his eyes rounding. "I didn't notice your face when we were outside. Where's the bus that hit you?"

"Yeah, that's a long story."

"That's what I'm here for. Long stories." He dropped his duffle next to the couch and looked around. "Nice place."

"Belongs to Avery's dad."

Ben's eyebrows rose and his expression said they'd talk about that later. Gabe nearly laughed out loud. Apparently Mac wasn't alone in her thoughts that it was unusual for exes to be friends. But, hey, even he and Mac had parted on good, albeit unsatisfactory, terms.

"Okay. So what's the situation?" Ben asked.

Gabe offered a fast rundown of the events that had them in hiding.

"I'm headed into Denver on Monday," Gabe said. "Surveillance of the employees entering the field office."

"I'd like to go, too," Mac said.

Gabe grimaced. "That's a very bad idea."

"I didn't ask for an opinion," she said.

"She's safer with us than here alone." Ben nodded toward the tall windows.

Was she? Gabe bit back a response. His brother didn't know Mac as well as he did. The woman was not a sideline player. That would make it difficult to keep her safe.

"Mind if we review the intel before we head into Denver?" Ben said. "I want to be sure I'm in the loop on everything."

"Sure," Gabe said.

Ben looked to Mac. "That okay with you?"

"She's already gone over everything multiple times. Maybe you and I…" Gabe stopped when his gaze met Mac's. He was doing his best to protect her from the emotional trauma of repeating her story yet again. Her face said she knew what he was doing and wouldn't be coddled.

"No," Mac said. "I don't mind. I think it would be good to have objective eyes on the information."

"Perfect," Ben returned. "We can do that early a.m."

A yawn slipped from Mac as she leaned against the couch, her head drooping.

"Mac, go get some sleep," Gabe said.

She straightened, her eyes widening. "I'm fine. Are we going to sleep in shifts?"

"Ben and I can handle security."

"I'm putting both of you at risk. I'll take a shift."

"Tell you what," Ben said. "If you wake up in the night, you can relieve one of us. Deal?"

Gabe watched the expression move across Mac's face and knew immediately that she'd agree to Ben's suggestion.

"Fair enough," she finally said.

Yeah. He probably ought to keep his mouth shut. It was clear she was on the defensive with him.

"Good night, then, gentlemen." She looked from him to Ben and slowly hobbled out of the room, with Winston following.

"Night, Mackenzie," Ben said.

There was silence in the little house as Mac left the room.

"What happened to Mackenzie's leg?" Ben asked.

"That's what started this journey. Mission gone wrong in Toronto. Mac's had a rough eight weeks."

"We have a lot of ground to cover tomorrow, don't we?" Ben observed. He paused. "Tell me again, why do you call her 'Mac'?"

"That's her name." Gabe frowned, wary of the question. "Mac. Mackenzie."

"Sure, I get that. The mascot of the Mack truck is a bulldog. She has a bulldog. *Whatever.* Still, she's a woman. No woman should be called Mac."

Stunned, Gabe could only stare at his brother. Seriously? The guy who went through girlfriends like breakfast cereal was giving him advice? "What do you know?" he sputtered. "You're not exactly a relationship expert."

"I know more than you, pal. And, by the way, from where I'm standing, you two sound like you're an old married couple."

"That's not funny." But as he said the words, Gabe's mind flashed back through the conversation since his brother's arrival and he cringed.

"I agree." Ben folded his arms over his chest.

"I guess Mac and I are both a little edgy," he admitted, eager to disprove his brother's theory. "We've been on the road since late last night, and in that time, someone's tried to kill us or sabotage us multiple times."

"I get that. But it's obvious that you still care for her."

"She's a friend. I care about all my friends."

"Right. A friend."

"I haven't seen her in five years."

"And yet, nothing has changed."

Silence fell as his brother eyed him. He knew Ben recalled how low Gabe had been when Mac broke things off five years ago. It wasn't a good time in his life, and he didn't want to repeat the scenario.

Ben shook his head. "Be very careful, Gabe."

"Always. Always," he repeated for himself more than for his brother.

"Mind if I ask why you were protecting her a few minutes ago?" Ben asked. "Why didn't you want her to give me the backstory?"

Gabe shoved his hands in his pockets and paced back and forth. "Look, Mac's got some PTSD. You saw her. She's a shadow of herself. Between the injuries and the stress of being on the run, I'm concerned."

"I get that, but this might be the time she remembers something that she didn't the other six times she talked about it."

"I know you're right. Just go easy on her."

"I'll take that under consideration." His brother glanced around the living area. "How come Avery let you use her house when you dumped her?"

Again, Gabe grimaced. There was no getting anything by his brother. "I didn't dump her. Merely pointed out that I couldn't give her what she wanted."

"What was that?"

"Promises."

"Promises. Okay, sure. You couldn't give her promises because you're still in love with Mackenzie."

The words, spoken matter-of-factly, hit their target with accuracy, and Gabe's head jerked back.

"Could you lower your voice?" he asked.

Lower your voice and put down your weapon was more like it. Gabe wasn't armed, and he definitely wasn't about to get into a semantics argument tonight. He cared for Mac. Friends cared for each other. Ben was way off base.

Unfazed, his brother rummaged in his duffle bag and removed a neatly folded stack of clothes. "I stopped by your place and got you a change of clothes and grabbed your spare glasses, as requested."

"Thanks."

"What happened to you, anyhow?" Once again, he assessed Gabe's face. "You look like you were in a bar fight."

"Car bomb in Phoenix."

"A car bomb. Seriously?" Ben's eyes widened at the information. "When was this?"

Gabe glanced at his watch. "Twenty-six hours ago. It was a rental-agency vehicle. The Lord and Mac's dog saved me from an untimely fate. As it was, we ended up driving to Colorado because of damage to my ears."

"How are you doing now?"

"I haven't given it much thought, so I guess it

is better. I'm picking up most sounds, except low pitches and mumbling."

"So you said you've been on the road since last night?"

"Yeah. Whoever wants Mac dead has attempted three times. If I hadn't been there, I wouldn't have believed it myself."

"What's the plan?"

"After you interview Mac, let's look at a time-line of events and see if we can generate some leads. No one has seen your face, and investigation is your forte."

"Give me your gut thoughts on the situation, Gabe. Why is she being targeted?"

"Mac most likely knows something that she doesn't know she knows."

"Or she's hiding something," Ben said.

"Hiding something?" Gabe recalled the kids searching the Crown Vic in Albuquerque. Was there something to that?

"You haven't seen the woman in five years. We have to look at every angle until we rule each one out." He paused. "You're okay with me nosing around into Mac's background? Her personal information?"

Gabe nodded, knowing his brother was right, which was why he'd called him. Ben could be brutally objective, while Gabe found himself wanting to defend Mac at every turn. Ben's plan was the only way to get to the bottom of things.

"You bring a weapon with you?" Ben asked.

"Yeah. Mac is carrying as well."

"Excellent." Ben glanced around and gave a slow shake of his head. "I don't like this setup."

"I'm not thrilled with it myself, but it was the best I could do on short notice."

"I've got a few contacts in the area. I'm going to try to locate a real safe house as soon as possible."

"Thanks," Gabe said.

"Mind if I do a recon of the place?" Ben asked.

"Let me go with you."

"No. I got it. You get some sleep. You look awful. I'll do the first watch."

"You sure?"

"Yeah. I brought paperwork with me I need to review."

"Okay. I'll set my alarm for four hours from now."

"How many bedrooms in this place, anyhow?" Ben asked. "I don't have to bunk with you, do I?"

Gabe's jaw sagged at the words and he recalled his joking comments to Mac about snoring. "What's that supposed to mean?"

"You snore, buddy."

"I do not. You're the one with the deviated septum. But there are four bedrooms. You can have your own or share with Winston," Gabe muttered as he turned to leave.

"Wait," Ben said. "Any food around here?"

"There's pizza in the fridge. We ordered extra, so help yourself."

"It's not pineapple, is it?"

Gabe chuckled, remembering his pizza discussion with Mac. Forty-eight hours since he'd been assigned this mission and now everything seemed to circle back to her.

"No pineapple," he said.

"Whew."

"Your annoying big-brother attitude aside, thanks for coming."

"That's what bros are for. Besides, I figured this would be a great time to once again emphasize all the reasons why you should join Denton Security and Investigations."

Uh-oh, the big pitch was about to begin again. In truth, every time Ben pitched, Gabe lost a little more resistance to the idea.

"Denton Security and Investigations. That's still the name you're going with?"

"Yeah, the family business. Although I am open to Denton Brothers. Which do you prefer?"

"I prefer you stop selling for five minutes." Gabe tried not to laugh. "The family business, huh? Is the general aware of the family business? I can just see his face turning red and the veins pulsing in his neck."

"I'll let him know eventually. He'll get over himself if we present a united front."

"Ben, you've been out of the military for six

months. How long do you think you can keep this from him?"

"He plays lots of golf these days. I'm good at least until the Thanksgiving interrogation."

"You're living dangerously." Living dangerously was an understatement. Gabe didn't want to be the one to face their father, though he could see the advantage of two of them approaching him.

"Maybe. But I wasn't talking about me. What are your thoughts on this?"

Gabe had plenty of thoughts, and most involved fear of leaving behind the only career he'd ever known. But he wasn't ready to be completely transparent with his brother, because once he did it was as good as a commitment.

"I've got a promotion coming up," Gabe said.

"There's always a promotion coming up. This is about being your own boss. Being part of something that's yours and not owned by Uncle Sam."

"I like my job."

"Great, because we're bidding on a few government contracts. You could have your freedom and your government job perks, too."

Gabe blinked at this answer. It sounded almost too good to be true, and he was once again tempted.

"What can I contribute to the family business, as you call it?" he asked.

"Plenty, with your experience. And we've been

talking about opening a branch in the west. Denver would be ideal."

"We, who?"

"I've brought in a few veterans—men and women formerly in the intelligence arena. Right now, we're focused on investigation, but I'd like to branch out into security. That's where you'd come in. Training, maybe. Like you do now."

"I don't know…" Gabe hedged.

"Just tell me that you'll think about it."

"Okay, sure. I'll think about it."

And he would. Gabe headed down the hall to one of the bedrooms as he considered his brother's offer.

The idea of moving to the private sector was both terrifying and intriguing.

He tossed the clothes Ben brought him on the bed and thought about Mac sleeping in the next room. What about living in the same city as her?

Yeah, that would be the terrifying part.

SEVEN

Mac yawned as she stood in front of the French press. She leaned against the kitchen counter and closed her eyes, inhaling the aroma of brewing coffee. "Four minutes," she murmured.

"What are you doing?"

"Huh?" Her eyes flew open, and she whirled around, planting her face into Gabe's chest.

She jumped away, gripping the counter to steady herself. Nothing like a little humiliation to immediately wake her up. He'd recently showered and changed clothes, and he smelled good. She'd forgotten just how good. Like soap and toothpaste and Gabe.

"Easy there." Amusement filled his eyes as he nodded toward the fancy coffee machine on the counter. "Why didn't you just use that?"

"Are you kidding? Look at all those buttons. It would have taken me an hour to figure it out. I need coffee now." A soft beep sounded, and Mac stopped the stove timer. "This takes four minutes."

She gently pressed the plunger on the French press until the filter reached the bottom of the beaker. "All done. Want some?"

"No, thanks. I like a challenge. I think I remember how this works."

"Good." Ben's voice rang out. "Then you can make me a cup, too."

The two joked and exchanged barbs as Gabe made coffee, leaving Mac an opportunity to observe the brothers.

Ben looked like a soldier, tall and lean, while Gabe was solid all over and a little nerdy around the edges with his black-framed glasses.

"Here you go," Gabe said as he slid a steaming mug on the table in front of his brother. "I'm taking my coffee with me. I promised Winston a stroll."

Ben sipped his coffee. Once the front door closed, he turned to Mac. "How are you doing, Mackenzie?"

"Better. I got a few hours of sleep in. Funny, how it's easier to sleep when I know there are people in the house who have my back."

"Sleep is good." He sipped his coffee and eyed her over the rim of the mug, a question in his eyes.

"What is it?" she asked.

"Gabe is concerned that discussing the mission in Toronto may trigger some mental-health issues."

The words gave her pause. Gabe had put himself into the role of her protector and she neither needed nor wanted one. Maybe if she wasn't a trained agent, she'd be flattered. Instead, she found herself annoyed. A healing leg injury was no reason to assume she couldn't take care of herself. She needed his help to figure out what was going on, not because she couldn't protect herself.

"Mackenzie?" Ben asked. "Are you okay?"

"Yes. I'm fine," she said. "To answer your question, Gabe could be right. I can't say for certain what response might be triggered, but I want to go ahead. I can't live like this. On the run. Not knowing who or why someone wants me dead. I want my life back."

"I agree with you, one hundred percent. The sooner we figure out why you're a liability to someone, the sooner we can target your unknown enemy."

"Thank you, Ben. I really appreciate your help." She searched for the right words. "I'm sorry we took you away from your job."

He shook his head. "I'm glad Gabe called me. And you're his friend, so I'm here for you as well."

Mac put her hands around her mug. "That's very generous of you, especially since I'm sure you must have some concerns about me."

"To be honest, it's Gabe I'm concerned about."

"Gabe?"

"He's still got feelings for you."

"No. No. It's nothing like that. We're partners

in this mission. Actually, I've tried several times to get him to leave. Go back to Washington. He promised Todd Shipman he'd get me to Denver. I'm here. His responsibility has ended."

"You have to realize that he's not here because of responsibility."

Mac crossed her arms and considered his words for a moment, before quickly discarding them. This was an assignment. She and Gabe were history.

"I think you're wrong," she finally said.

"We can agree to disagree."

She could only smile at that. "The Denton brothers are a lot alike."

"Are we?" Ben chuckled. "Gabe's a good guy. I can tell you that." He paused and cocked his head. "I'm trying to lure him to the private sector. If it comes up, maybe you can put in a good word for Denton Security and Investigations."

"I can do that." She finished off her coffee. "Tell me about your company. I have to admit that I would have pegged you for a lifer when it came to the military."

"A year ago, I would have agreed with you."

"What happened?"

"I took a look at myself in the mirror and didn't like what I saw. I wasn't happy, and I couldn't remember why I was doing a job that didn't fulfill me."

She nodded, well able to relate. While in hiding for the last few weeks, she had begun to think about her career path, her loyalty and her future. Would she have the courage to veer from the known to the unknown, like Ben had? Like he wanted Gabe to? She wasn't sure yet.

"I've made a lot of contacts, and that's provided a good foundation for the company. We've got more business than I can handle."

"What is it that you do?"

"Right now, white-collar investigations, but I'm ready to expand into security. Domestic. I'd want to recruit Gabe to handle the security side. I can't expand without someone I trust partnering with me."

"Gabe would be perfect for the job."

"Yeah, I think so, too."

The sound of the front door opening and closing had both Mac and Ben on alert. Winston raced into the room ahead of Gabe. Tongue lolling, he ran in a circle, pleased with himself.

"What are you two talking about?" Gabe asked. He opened the refrigerator and took out a bottle of water.

"You," Ben said.

"I figured as much." He downed the water and leaned against the refrigerator. "This guy gave me a workout. We ran through the woods to the east of the house."

"What's it look like out there?" Ben asked.

"There are a few trails that lead out to the highway." He pulled a few brambles and leaves from his jeans. "Very overgrown."

"Another reason to get out of here soon. This place is too accessible," Ben said, his voice tense. "I'll have a place set up by Monday night."

"Are we ready to get started?" Gabe asked.

Mac nodded. "Do you mind if we sit in the kitchen? It's easier for me to get up and down from a straight-backed chair."

"Sure."

"I want to be clear, Ben," Gabe said. "What we're doing here is a completely off-book operation. We're trying to determine who the mole is at the Agency in Denver and why Mac is being targeted."

Ben nodded as his brother continued.

"We've been unofficially provided a window of time to figure this out before the Agency will no doubt be forced to take action with intel that supposedly implicates Mac in the bank job in Toronto and then by association the explosion at Polson Pier."

Ben nodded. "The bank account that was opened in her name."

"Yeah," Gabe returned. "Which would signal the FBI and Department of Homeland Security, who would begin an internal investigation."

"Understood. Let's start at the beginning," Ben said. "Gabe gave me a quick briefing, Mackenzie. But I want to hear it in your own words. Tell me everything that happened before Toronto."

"This is a highly classified, need-to-know op," Gabe said.

"Look, Boy Scout, you contacted me. If I'm going to help Mackenzie, I need to know."

Mac's eyes rounded at the interaction between brothers. So she wasn't the only one who'd noticed Gabe's propensity for following the rules. He only glared at Ben.

"Gabe, your brother is right. The advantage here is Ben can be objective and hopefully see things that I've missed."

"I know. I know," Gabe said. "This is just new territory for me."

"I get that," Ben said. "But someone on the inside is gunning for both of you. You don't have a choice, except to color outside the lines." He turned to Mac. "Go ahead."

"I was read in on the case in early spring. The bank robbery had just happened. Three dead guards."

"Why was the Agency interested in this incident?"

"They'd been monitoring a sleeper cell in Denver and activity indicated that funds from the Toronto bank job were funneled to an account managed by the leaders of the cell."

"How much are we talking?" Ben asked.

"Twenty million, though only one million showed up in the account. The rest is unaccounted for." She shared the details without emotion.

These were the facts, and as a professional she'd learned long ago to compartmentalize in an effort to remain objective.

Gabe's brother offered a low whistle. "That's a lot of reasons to want you dead."

Mac released a breath at his words. He was right. There were nineteen million reasons to want her dead.

"Why were you chosen for this assignment?"

"I'm fluent in French, and I'm based in Denver. Shipman sent me to meet with a potential asset. A roommate of the missing bank guard. The asset agreed to provide information in return for a visa into the US."

Ben nodded. "I'm just tossing out ideas, but is it possible you were chosen for another reason?"

"Another reason?" The question flustered her for a moment.

"I'd say anything is possible." Yes. Anything was possible. Her mind raced at the thought. Had she been played? Set up in an elaborate plot as the fall guy? The idea both terrified and angered her.

"Go ahead," Ben prompted.

"I...um." Mac cleared her throat and worked to tuck the premise Ben suggested into its own box so she could focus on his questions.

"Are you okay?" Gabe asked.

"Yes." She gave a firm nod. "Once I established that the asset had credible intel, we set up the meeting. Evaluating that information would determine the next step."

"Who else was involved in this mission?"

"Several analysts monitored the case, and Elizabeth Morrow was brought in and accompanied me to Toronto."

"Morrow. How well did you know her?"

"We weren't exactly friends. Liz is a loner." Mac paused and looked at Gabe and then away. "Yes, I know I'm considered a loner," she added. "But Liz, she's in a different category. We'd gone through training together and we've been together on a few missions, but I have to say, she isn't a talker. I know more about the barista at my local coffee shop than I do about Liz. However, I always thought we had a good working relationship."

"She never talked about growing up or her parents when you were working together?" Gabe asked. "Her file says she lost her parents when she was a freshman in college."

"I know what her file says. I asked for it when Shipman debriefed me. But there was one odd incident. I ran into her around the holidays, here in Denver, over a year ago. She's based here as well." Mac took a breath. "I was at a local restaurant getting takeout. Liz was sitting at the bar and I got the impression she'd been there a while drinking. I asked her if she was going home for Christmas. Liz said she didn't have a home, and that she was raised in foster care. She looked me right in the eye and said I had no idea what that was like."

Mac frowned, recalling the incident with regret. She should have tried harder to push past her own fears to connect with Liz on an emotional level.

"That was it?" Ben asked.

"No. When we were in Toronto, somehow family came up again. I think she brought up the embassy bombing. I hadn't read her file at that point, and I mentioned that she told me once that she was raised in foster care. Liz became really agitated, and raised her voice, telling me I didn't know what I was talking about." Mac paused. Recalling the incident continued to disturb her. She glanced between Gabe and Ben.

"It was as though she was another person. Then she gave me the verbatim story that's in her file about her parents dying when she was in college."

Mac shook her head. The incident had left her second-guessing herself. Now, she realized that it was a huge red flag and she should have listened to her gut. She wasn't imagining things.

What was the truth about Liz's past? And did it affect the events that unfolded with the mission? Was there a connection she was missing?

"That's very strange. Did you trust Morrow?" Ben asked.

"That's my job. To trust my team. Although, right now, I'm starting to think that every person attached to the task force could be culpable." She raised a brow. "Should that old saying apply to operatives?"

"What saying?" Gabe asked.

"No honor among thieves. I'm starting to think it's true." She sighed and tapped her foot nervously on the floor, then detailed how the Polson Pier dead drop had gone bad.

"Tell me about your informant," Ben said. He reached for the notebook on the table and tore out a piece of paper. "Any idea what information he had?"

"Abrak Taher was his name. He claimed that he had the hard drive of a computer that was jointly used by several roommates in the apartment, including James Smith, the American bank guard. It was never recovered."

Gabe turned to his brother. "Ben, you should know that on Friday, Shipman received intel indicating that Morrow may be alive and held hostage. Shipman asked Mac to come in to protect her," he said. "I'm beginning to wonder if whoever has Morrow used her to lure Mac out of hiding."

"So, if the intel is correct, Morrow didn't die on the pier." Ben made a note on the paper. "How far has the Agency gotten with tracking her down?"

"Nowhere, as far as we know," Mac said.

"Mackenzie, have you considered the possibility that Morrow was the inside person?" Ben asked.

"I've considered that everyone was an inside person." She'd been awake night after night trying to figure out who had set her up and why. "If it was Liz, then she was working with someone else at the Agency," Mac continued.

"What makes you think that?" Gabe asked.

"The GPS on you, for one. That IT staffer was working at someone's direction, someone with system admin access who could help them slide under the radar."

"You're right," Gabe said. "But that staffer is the direct link to our answers."

"Yeah, I agree," Ben said. "Did either of you get a visual on the guy in the black truck or the commercial moving truck?" Ben asked.

"Not close enough to be helpful," Gabe said. "We don't even know if both drivers are the same person."

Ben looked at Mac. "Could he…they be the guard from Toronto or the shooter on the pier?"

"It's impossible to say," she returned. "Neither Gabe nor I can ID the drivers. And I wasn't close enough in Toronto to provide a positive ID on a man who for the most part was hidden beneath his hat and sunglasses. Afterward, I didn't want to think about him." She didn't admit that for the last eight weeks, the shooter at the pier had kept in the shadows of her nightmares. Thinking about him when she was awake wasn't something she'd dared to do up to now.

"Could you think about him now?" Ben asked gently.

"I can try."

The only sound in the kitchen was the hum of the refrigerator. Mac said a silent prayer before she closed her eyes. She went back to the pier, back to that day. A shiver ran over her arms, and she licked her dry lips. She had to remember. Her life depended on remembering something about this shooter.

She visualized him, his face covered to his nose by a black neck gaiter and his head hidden by a black cap, the eyes anonymous behind dark aviators. He raised the rifle without hesitancy. Then, his left hand moved to lift the brim of his cap, his right index finger never leaving the trigger.

"Tattoo," Mac said. Her eyes popped open, and she gasped at the same time.

"What?" Gabe asked.

Mac wiped away the bead of perspiration that had formed on her upper lip. "He had a tattoo on his left forearm. Something circular." She blinked. "A lion's head."

"Bingo," Ben said. "I have a friend who can check the FBI tattoo recognition database. It may yield something that could help us." He looked at Mac and offered a nod of approval. "And I'll see what I can find out about Morrow's background."

They were one step closer, yet fear bubbled up inside of Mac. For eight weeks, she'd been running, always on the defensive, to stay alive. Now they were about to go on the offensive, straight to the enemy. Was she prepared for the consequences?

"You okay back there, Mac?" Gabe asked. He checked the rearview mirror of Ben's rental, glancing to where she and Winston sat in the back. "You're looking a little stressed."

"She has to be worn out from yesterday's interrogation," Ben said from the front passenger seat. "I know I am."

"Are you sure this is the right way?" Mac asked. "You haven't lived in Denver in a while."

"Nice try," Gabe said. Mac was an expert at evasion, and he was determined to call her on it, every single time. He hadn't done that five years ago, but instead had allowed her to continue to build her wall. The wall that eventually destroyed their relationship.

Gabe met her gaze in the mirror once again. "That wasn't the answer to my question," he said. "But, yeah, I know where I'm going."

Ben snickered. "The guidance thinks you missed your turn, too."

Gabe gave his brother the side-eye. "Thanks for the support there, big brother."

Ben raised his hands in response. "Just saying. The guidance doesn't lie."

"I'm doing some diversionary tactics to ensure we aren't being tailed," Gabe said.

Ben turned to her and winked. "Translation. He's lost."

Mac laughed, her voice warming Gabe. He'd gladly volunteer to be the target of all their jokes if it meant hearing her relaxed laughter more often.

"Make a right up ahead," she said. "It's a one-way street. Then circle back to Santa Fe."

"Nothing much changes in Denver, does it?" Gabe observed. It seemed as if he'd never left the Mile High City.

"Sure it does," Mac said. "You've passed at least four new businesses. The Colorado Ballet relocated down here to the arts district a while back. That's newish."

"Were you raised in Denver, Mackenzie?" Ben asked.

"Mostly. My family moved overseas when I hit high school."

"That's right. Gabe told me your father was an ambassador."

Gabe shot his brother a warning look. This wasn't the time to bring up a subject that might trigger the memories associated with her parents' deaths.

"What?" Ben returned.

"Gabe," Mac said gently, "it's all right. I'm almost thirty-four. I can talk about my parents without breaking down."

"Did I put my foot in my mouth again?" Ben asked, his gaze going from Gabe to Mac in the back seat.

"No. You're fine," Mac said. "When I was a freshman in high school, my father took the ambassador post."

"So no moving every three years like we did?" Ben continued.

"No," she said.

"We moved six times while we were growing up," Gabe interjected. "The only good part was Ben always had my back, and I had his."

"I always wished I had a brother or sister," Mac said. "Although, Megan and Lance Shipman are like siblings to me."

"It's got its advantages and disadvantages," Ben said. "We'll have to compare notes sometime. I know all Gabe's secrets."

"Cut it out, Ben," Gabe said. He was half-serious. Ben did know all his secrets, and a few could really cement the fact that he really was a nerd.

"There." Mac waved a hand into the front seat. "You just passed the field office."

"Yeah. I know. I was here on Friday. Remember?" Gabe said.

This time it was Ben who shot *him* a look. With the raising of his eyebrows and the quirking of his lips, Gabe recalled his comment about him and Mac acting like they were married.

He took a deep breath and resisted the urge to give his brother's shoulder a shove. "I'll go around the corner, and Ben and I can get out," Gabe said instead. He glanced around. "That bakery across the street from the entrance is a good location to watch for my IT tech buddy."

"Gabe, remind me what the target looks like," Ben said.

"Tall, lanky, Caucasian male. Dark, curly hair, glasses. Approximately twenty-five." Gabe shrugged. "No distinguishing marks."

"Got it." Ben glanced around. "I'll be at the bus stop."

"What about me?" Mac asked.

"What about you?" Gabe returned. "We're trying to keep you safe, so keep circling the block, but don't be obvious."

"Don't be obvious?" She practically snorted at his words. "I'm the one who's been in the field. Remember?"

"Sorry about that," Gabe said. The irony of the situation didn't escape him. Here he was back in the field again. He hoped it was like riding a bike.

"Everyone on comms?" Ben asked as Gabe pulled the vehicle to the curb.

"Yes," Mac said. She connected her headphones to the burner phone.

"Yeah." Gabe put the wireless earbuds into his ear and then dialed his brother's phone. "Okay, let's do this."

Ben was first to depart. He circled the rear of the sedan, glancing up and down the street. Gabe opened his door and stepped into the street. Around him, 7:00 a.m. traffic had begun to pick up, as the RTD, Denver's transit buses and light rail, moved early-morning commuters into the city from the burbs.

When Mac got out of the car, Gabe tapped the brim of her ball cap as she headed to the driver's seat to replace him. "Be careful," he murmured.

Her blue eyes met his, and a sweet smile curved her mouth. Gabe's heart stuttered.

"Me?" She shook her head. "I've been ordered to remain in the vehicle."

"You're also the one someone is trying to kill." The one who should have stayed in Bluebell away from potential danger.

Winston barked as if he'd read Gabe's mind.

"I've got protection sitting in the back seat," Mac continued.

His gaze swept her features, memorizing the round eyes and full lips. He leaned near enough to smell the mint on her breath. Any other situation and he'd take a chance and close the distance between them.

But this wasn't the time or the place to consider the risks of letting Mac into his heart.

"Don't take any chances, okay? I'd like to see you again. In one piece."

She placed a hand on his arm and looked up at him, her eyes warm with something he didn't want to analyze. "Ditto, pal."

With a final look at the vehicle before he turned

the corner, Gabe said a quick prayer. "Keep her safe, Lord."

Long strides took him down the street to the popular bakery and coffee shop, where Gabe ordered a plain joe and a scone to fit in with the urban crowd moving in and out of the place. He sat at a table next to the window, pretending to check his phone with rabid devotion, like every other patron. His position provided a perfect view of the field office.

The building was nondescript brick with no signage to identify the tenants. It might appear empty to the undiscerning eye, but it held the offices of the domestic division, at least as of his visit Friday. There were no windows on the first few floors, and when the front doors pushed open, two security guards were visible in the building's entry, monitoring everything that went in and out of the building.

"I've got eyes on the building from the bakery," Gabe said.

"Ten-four. I'm at the bus stop to your left," Ben said.

"Mac, you all right?" Gabe asked when Mac failed to respond.

"Yes. Yes. Winston needed a break."

Behind Gabe, loud laughter broke through the buzz of chatter as a group of women entered the bakery. Behind the women, two young men slipped into the shop.

"I've got him. Target just entered the bakery," Gabe said.

There was no doubt at all that the kid who walked in was the IT staffer who'd given him the security card a few days ago. Gabe stepped in the tech's path and crossed his arms over his chest, doing his best to appear menacing.

"Hey, how's it going?" Gabe asked.

"I…uh…" The kid's Adam's apple bobbed, and his eyes darted around. He was clearly desperate to escape.

"That good, huh?"

The guy who came in with the tech puffed out his own chest and frowned. "Ribinoff, you know this guy?"

"Sure he knows me. I met Ribinoff on Friday," Gabe said. "You gave me my badge and security card. Right?"

The other guy narrowed his gaze. He looked from Ribinoff to Gabe. "Have we met?"

"We are right now. Gabe Denton. I'm here from DC to handle a special project for Senior Officer Todd Shipman." He frowned. "You know Shipman, right?"

Both men paled at the mention of Todd Shipman.

"I'm in serious trouble," Ribinoff mumbled. He shoved a table toward Gabe, startling the patrons as he bumped into people in line and sped out the doors, knocking over a trash receptacle as he made a hard left.

Gabe followed, pushing open the glass doors

and racing onto the sidewalk. "He's on the move. Heading north."

"Eyes on him," Ben said.

"Kid's name is Ribinoff."

The tech then crossed the street with a quick dash through traffic, over and around cars. Horns blared as he dodged a city dump truck.

"He's fast," Gabe said.

"You got this, old man," Ben said in his ear.

Gabe trailed him, then he stopped and looked to his rear. Someone was following him. He was sure of it.

"He's yours, Ben. I've got a tail."

"Be careful," his brother said.

"I'm coming up the street from the other direction," Mac said.

"No. Mac," Gabe said, unable to hold back his irritation and concern. "You're supposed to stay in the car."

"I'm a CIA operations officer. I don't stay put in cars," she said. "I'll be at your back door in five minutes."

Gabe ducked into an alley and picked up speed until he passed a dumpster. Then he stayed out of view, crouching against the wall behind the metal container. The hard, rough edges of the brick poked at his back through his shirt as he waited.

Moments later, he heard heavy breathing.

Whoever had followed him was definitely a civilian with the stealth skills of a large animal. From the sound of his footfalls, he was at least two hundred and fifty pounds, and panting to keep up as well.

When the guy passed the dumpster, Gabe jumped out and pinned him against the wall.

Yeah, he was a big guy, all right. Big and out of shape, a white male, in his late thirties, with short blond hair, wearing a T-shirt and jeans.

He swung a massive fist toward Gabe.

And missed.

Gabe landed a blow to the guy's gut.

He crumpled, but quickly rebounded to elbow Gabe hard and pin him to the wall next to the dumpster, knocking the Bluetooth from his ears.

"Who are you?" Gabe asked while the guy pushed him into the unyielding brick.

"I'm the guy who's going to kill you unless you tell me where Mackenzie Sharp is."

"Why do you want Sharp?"

"Because she has our money."

"What?" Gabe jerked back, working to push the weight off him. "Whose money?" His thoughts flashed to the attempted carjacking in Albuquerque. He fought to keep his thoughts objective, to stay focused, though he couldn't deny all the indicators pointing at Mac.

The guy tightened his hold on Gabe and his face reddened with anger. "Ask Sharp. She has the money."

"What about Morrow?" Gabe asked. "Is Morrow alive?"

"She died on that pier in Toronto, and I'm thinking Sharp killed her. Last thing Liz said to me before she went to Toronto was that Sharp double-crossed her and had the money. *Our money.*"

For a moment, Gabe froze. Mac and Morrow working together? He didn't believe it. Couldn't let himself believe it.

A surge of anger at the implication was all it took for Gabe to slip from the guy's grasp and grab his arm, twisting it behind him. "That's why you're trying to kill Sharp?"

"What are you talking about?" he panted. "We don't want her dead…yet. We just want our money."

"We? Who's we?"

The guy gave a vigorous shake of his head. "I told you way more than I should."

Gabe pulled the guy's arm higher.

"Oww," he yelled. "Okay. Okay. Ease up. 'We' is me and Ribinoff."

"So that was you in Phoenix and Tucson," Gabe returned. It seemed the more information he got, the more confused the situation became. "I thought you said you didn't want Sharp dead."

"Nope, not me. I didn't start following you until Tucson. That van thing, in the rest stop? I saw it, but it wasn't me. I can claim responsibility for trying to jack your Crown Vic in Albuquerque. Just looking for what's mine, dude."

The Bluetooth on the ground vibrated, causing Gabe to turn his head and loosen his hold briefly.

"Get. Off. Me," the guy screamed. He pushed himself off the wall and threw his full weight against Gabe.

As the two flew across the alley, his elbow struck Gabe's face, knocking off his glasses.

"That was unnecessary," Gabe muttered to the blurry and retreating form racing down the alley, kicking up loose bits of gravel on the way.

Before the guy reached the end of the alley, the muffled sound of a gunshot filled the morning air.

"What?" Gabe's pulse pounded out of control, as he rolled out of the middle of the alley and pressed himself flat against the wall. He made a frantic search of the windows and the roof. No sign of the shooter.

Minutes passed.

"You shot him?"

Gabe looked up to see Ben standing over him. "He was hit?"

"Yeah."

"No, I didn't shoot him." Gabe grabbed his glasses and the Bluetooth earpiece from the gravel before doing another visual sweep of the area.

"Somebody did," Ben said as Gabe struggled to his feet.

"You get Ribinoff?" Gabe asked.

"That kid is part monkey. Scrambled over a wall and took off." Ben shook his head as the two raced down the alley to the body.

Gabe crouched down and checked for a pulse

on the big guy, who was facedown on the ground in a puddle of blood. He shook his head. "Whoever hit him was a professional. A single shot." His eyes searched the buildings that formed the alley. Plenty of windows. Plenty of opportunity.

"Yeah," Ben agreed. He slipped two fingers into the man's back pocket and pulled out a wallet. "Meet Wade Masterson."

"Masterson. Doesn't ring a bell."

"I'll check his background," Ben said.

"Thanks."

"You want to tell me what happened when you went off comms?" Ben asked.

"He took a swing at me."

"No, Gabe," Ben said. "I know you, and something else happened."

Gabe looked at his brother. It wasn't that he didn't trust him, but repeating what Masterson said out loud would make it real and he was still stunned by the information. He hoped he could make it disappear.

"Gabe?"

"Masterson talked before he was shot. He said that Morrow was connected to the stolen money."

"Morrow?" Ben's eyes popped at the info. He nodded slowly. "Okay. That makes everything fall into place. She's the inside person."

"There's more." Gabe hesitated, dreading what he was about to say. "He indicated that Mac was involved as well and that she's responsible for

Morrow's death." He shook his head and released a breath. It was almost a relief to be able to share the information with someone else.

"Your agency says Morrow is alive." Ben shook his head. "What about Mackenzie being involved? Do you believe him?"

"Come on. You know I'm in an impossible situation here." An understatement at best. He had an obligation to follow up on the intel, no matter what he believed. Ben knew that as well as he did.

"What do you want me to do?" Ben asked.

"I'm going to need you to dig a little deeper into both Mac and her partner's activities for the last eight weeks. Probably longer."

"You got it." Ben paused. "You didn't answer me. Do you believe him? I mean, about Mackenzie?"

"I don't know what to believe, and it's tearing me up."

"What happened?" Mac asked as she approached them from the other end of the alley with Winston.

Both Ben and Gabe turned at the sound of her voice.

"You were supposed to stay in the car," Gabe barked. "There's a shooter out there." Again, his gaze spanned the buildings looming over them. Masterson had been shot. Mac would be an easy target. "At least stay against the wall."

Mac raised a hand. "Easy, Gabe." Then she pressed her back against the brick and offered him a tissue from her messenger bag. "Ah, your nose is bleeding."

Gabe nodded his begrudging thanks and wiped the blood from his face.

"Mackenzie, do you recognize this guy?" Ben asked. He examined Wade Masterson's left arm. "No tattoo."

"No. Are we going to leave him?" she asked.

"That's the plan," Gabe said. "There's nothing we can do here."

"I'll call 911 with one of the burner phones," Mac said.

"Okay, but we need to get out of here. Now. And stay on comms," Gabe returned.

"Where's the car?" Ben asked as they headed out the other end of the alley.

"Two blocks down. Some guy pulled out, and I snapped up the spot."

"I'll keep my eye on Mackenzie," Ben said. Head down, he crossed the street.

Gabe kept to the right of the sidewalk, with Mac and Winston a distance behind. He began to process Wade Masterson's words. *Sharp has the money.*

Each footfall on the cement beat the words into his brain.

Sharp has the money.

Sharp has the money.

The compelling words of the dead man continued to shake Gabe's confidence in Mac's innocence, and he hated himself for his thoughts.

"I don't see the car," Ben said.

Gabe's head jerked up, startling him from his reverie.

"It's right..." Mac gasped, the sound echoing in his ear. "The car is gone."

As they approached the open parking spot along the curb, she let out a breath and stared down where glass littered the ground. Then she turned and walked over to the storefront window behind them and feigned interest in the display.

"It's a rental," Ben said. "It's insured, and there wasn't anything of value inside." He walked to the corner and pressed the pedestrian button at the crosswalk.

"I can't believe it," Gabe said.

"Let's face it," Mac said. "Since Toronto, everything I touch turns into a dumpster fire."

Ben cleared his throat. "I'll call the rental agency to get another vehicle, then file a police report. This is going to take a while."

"We'll find a way back to the house," Gabe said.

"Are you sure?"

"Yeah."

"Stay safe," Ben said. His gaze connected with Gabe's for a long moment in an unspoken message that said, *Watch your back.*

Gabe nodded, though his brother was already gone.

"We just need to get back to Bluebell without anyone following us," Mac said.

"Any suggestions?" Gabe asked.

"I've got a ride-share app on my personal phone," she said.

"That's forty miles. You have cash, but do you have a disposable credit card?"

"Yes," Mac said. "Plenty of cash and cards."

An ominous dread filled him at her words. Gabe turned on the sidewalk and stared at Mac as she stood beneath the awning of a local business with Winston at her side. She patted her messenger bag and smiled.

At the gesture, his stomach turned. He debated telling her what Masterson said in the alley and decided to wait. Wait and see. For what, he didn't know. Mac's vindication, perhaps?

"Gabe?"

"I hear you. Let's go. We have a lot to process."

That much was true. Maybe the only truth.

Gabe worked to comprehend the possibility that everything he'd thought was the truth when he landed in Denver on Friday and met with Shipman could be a lie.

Logic reminded him that, at minimum, Mac deserved his trust until she was proven guilty. The problem was the clues were starting to be stacked against her. The offshore account and now a dead man's confession.

The only thing certain was that Gabe didn't have a clue what he was going to do next.

EIGHT

"Have you heard from Ben?" Mac asked. She filled a glass with water from the tap, pausing to glance outside, where dusk had settled, before she eased into a chair at the kitchen table. "I thought he was coming back here after he took care of the rental car. It's almost dark. Should we be concerned?"

Gabe's back was to her as he waited on the coffee machine. "Ben can handle himself. Right now, he's reaching out to his contacts, and running checks on the Ribinoff kid and Masterson." He stared out the kitchen window without turning toward her.

Mac nodded. "Who do you think shot Wade Masterson?" The question had plagued her all afternoon, though she hadn't said anything.

"Someone who didn't want him talking to me," Gabe said.

She frowned. Had she imagined the edge to his

voice? Maybe he was concerned about Ben, but was trying to hide it.

For a few minutes she was quiet, as she turned over the events of the morning in her head.

"I don't get it," she finally said. "We keep adding more players, but we don't seem to be able to figure out what's going on or where Liz is. Nothing makes sense."

"No. It doesn't." The words were flat and without emotion.

Mac rubbed her arms against the chill in the room.

Something had shifted since the incident in Denver this morning, and she didn't know what. Gabe's easy banter and amusing comments were all but gone. Several times, she felt his gaze on her. She'd look up to find that he was watching her.

Weighing. Measuring. Why?

"We're on the outside looking in without the Agency resources," Mac said. "If we could connect with Shipman without the inside person finding out, we might be able to stop this cat-and-mouse game."

Once again, Gabe was silent.

Winston padded into the room, the soft jingling of his collar and tags alerting her to his presence. He put his big head on her lap and looked up at her with his soulful eyes, begging for attention. Mac complied and rubbed his velvety ears. At least the bulldog still liked her.

Frustrated, Mac cleared her throat. "What's going on, Gabe?" she asked. The words slipped from her lips before she had a chance to consider the wisdom of the question.

Gabe turned from the counter. His hazel eyes searched her face, though he didn't respond.

But Winston did.

The bulldog barked and moved to the kitchen door. Snout pressed against the glass, he released a low, ominous growl.

Gabe dropped to the floor. "Get down, Mac! That dog can sense danger. We need to pay attention."

"Come here, boy," she commanded. Winston was at her side in a heartbeat.

As she, too, moved to the floor, the sound of glass shattering had both Mac and Gabe jumping.

Mac held Winston by the collar as she turned to see razor-sharp shards of glass hanging from the kitchen window over the sink.

"Our shooter is back and he's closer than those woods," Gabe said. "I'm guessing he was waiting for nightfall. We have to get out of here. Now. Before he gets any closer."

"Can we make it to the minivan?" Mac asked.

"We better try." He tossed her the keys. "I'll distract him. Head out the front door and don't stop."

She nodded and reached for Winston's leash from where it dangled on a kitchen chair. "Okay, but I'm not going anywhere without you." Mac scooted on her bottom to the living room, where she grabbed her messenger bag. Using the couch arm as leverage, she stood. There was no way she could crawl out the front door. Her leg simply would not bend that far yet.

Gabe stood as well and inched along the wall to one of the bedrooms. A moment later, she heard a window opening, and a gun blast followed by return fire.

Yet another shot rang out as Mac exited the house with Winston at her side. In the gravel drive, the pitiful minivan, with its blown-out rear window, now had four slashed tires.

Mac pulled out her Glock and moved quickly behind the branches of a wide blue spruce with Winston. With only the rising moon to illuminate the area, she waited for Gabe.

One. Two more shots sounded. Then, in the distance, the wailing of police sirens could be heard, coming closer.

"Come on, Gabe. Come on," she murmured. Her heart banged in her chest, the sound getting louder and louder, along with her anxiety. "Oh, Lord, please, keep him safe."

A moment later, the door opened, and Mac released a small gasp at the sight of Gabe racing across the drive to her, kicking up gravel as he moved.

"What's happening?" she asked.

He caught his breath and glanced around. "Gunshot sounds carry pretty far. One of the neighbors must have called the police."

"Where's the shooter?"

"I don't know. My guess is that whoever is out there heard the sirens and is retreating. Hopefully, they're going to be on the other side of the woods. But there's no way to be certain."

"What do you want to do?" she asked.

Gabe turned to look at the house, thinking. "I tried to reach Ben, but he didn't pick up. We'll hitch a ride to a public place and then call him again."

"Okay," Mac said.

"There's a trail behind us," Gabe said. "Let's go. Fast."

"I don't do fast," she said.

Gabe frowned. "You do now. Get on my back."

"You must be joking." She stared at him in the fading light.

"Get on my back."

"What about my cane?"

"Leave it. We can get another."

Mac glanced at the woods to the east of the house and then at Gabe, anxiety rising. "You can't carry me through there."

"This isn't a discussion. Get on." Gabe stooped down and Mac positioned herself on his back, holding tight to his shoulders.

"Winston. Come," Mac commanded. The bulldog followed them into the darkness, where the trees enveloped them.

Mac tucked her head into his shirt, narrowly avoiding a branch. "How can you see?"

"I've hiked the trail a few times and walked Winston through here."

"Not with a body on your back."

"You're a lightweight." He said the words without pause.

"If you say so," Mac murmured. She raised her face, only to have her cheek slapped by the brush and her ball cap plucked from her head. Mac released a small sound of surprise as the cap disappeared.

"What?" Gabe asked, not breaking stride.

"Nothing. Nothing." Caps were replaceable. She tucked her head down again and tightened her grip on his shoulders as he passed through a narrow path.

Minutes later, Mac heard the rhythmic whooshing and thumping of cars driving on the highway.

"I hear vehicles," she said.

"Yeah. It won't be busy this time of night. That will help. The problem is going to be flagging someone down in the dark."

"There's a flashlight in my bag," Mac said.

"Ah, the messenger bag," Gabe mumbled.

Mac noted his odd comment but said nothing.

Gabe stopped at the edge of the wooded area and crouched down to let her off his back. Then he pointed to the grassy incline that led to the road below. "We need to slide down there to the highway." He looked at her. "Think you can do that?"

"Yes." She'd do whatever it took at this point.

"Okay, I'll take Winston and go first." He half walked, half ran down the incline, and then called Winston, while gently clapping his hands. "Come on, boy. Come on."

The dog whined and looked at Mac.

"You can do it, Winston," she said, giving him a small nudge.

Winston barked and raced into Gabe's arms like a kid on a slide.

"Your turn, Mac," he called.

Mac assessed the angle of the incline before she sat on the ground and inched her way down, managing to get caught on shrubbery twice along the way. If she kept her injured leg raised, it wasn't painful, merely embarrassing.

At the bottom of the incline, Gabe held out a hand and pulled her up. She bumped into his chest and froze before awkwardly stepping away to brush dirt from her backside and legs.

"Flashlight?" he said.

Mac unzipped the messenger bag and rummaged inside. "Here you go." She handed Gabe the flashlight.

"You and Winston wait there behind the guardrail. I'll flag someone down."

Traffic was slow on a Monday evening, as he'd

predicted. A few cars zipped past, and an occasional truck. When a large produce truck rumbled around the corner, Gabe stepped into the road and waved the flashlight.

The pneumatic hissing of the truck's brakes competed with the vehicle's horn as the driver pulled to the shoulder of the road. The driver leaned over to the passenger side, and the window opened. "You okay, pal?" he called out.

"My wife and I have a disabled vehicle on the other side of the woods. Can you give us a lift down the road?"

"Sure."

When the driver leaned over to push open the passenger door, the light from inside the cab illuminated his smiling, weathered face. "I'm Harley."

A friendly face. The man's demeanor alone was enough to slow Mac's breathing.

"Gabe and Mackenzie," Gabe said.

Gabe helped Mac over the guardrail, and she held his arm in a death grip, determined not to trip and fall in the darkness.

Harley frowned and looked at Winston trailing behind. "He bite?"

"Not unless I tell him to," Mac said.

That elicited a hearty laugh from the trucker. "Fair enough."

"Mac," Gabe said quietly next to her ear. "I'm going to boost you into the cab and then Winston."

"I can do this." And she would. She'd had

enough awkwardness for one day, riding on Gabe's back. Holding on to the frame of the door, Mac used her right leg to step up and raised her left leg slowly into the cab. "Got it."

"You hurt that leg, little lady?" Harley asked.

"It's an old injury. No big deal."

"Here comes Winston," Gabe said. He hoisted the bulldog by his posterior until he was on Mac's lap.

"Come on up here, puppy," Mac murmured while Gabe jumped into the truck next to her. When his leg touched hers, Mac inched away. Nearly shot and killed, and then embarrassed to death. That's how she'd remember today.

"Where you headed?" Harley asked. He glanced into his mirrors and signaled.

"Depends," Gabe said. "Where's the nearest truck stop?"

"Oh, there's a place about twenty miles from here."

"Perfect, could you drop us off?" Gabe returned.

"Surely."

Winston raised his head and glared at Harley, his upturned jaw and drooping eyes almost comical. Then he shifted to grace Mac with a generous and slobbery kiss.

"Maybe you'd be more comfortable with your dog in the back seat," the trucker said.

Mac glanced at the extended cab's second row of seats. Yes, that was an excellent idea in theory, but her leg wouldn't be happy, and Winston wouldn't be persuaded without her.

"He won't leave me," she said.

"That might get uncomfortable," Harley said.

"Tell me about it." She sighed and wiped her cheek as Winston settled on her lap, his wrinkled face nestled in the crook of her arm.

Gabe looked at her and frowned. "I can hold Winston."

"It's okay. We've done this before."

From around the bend in the road, two police cars appeared, racing in the opposite direction, their sirens loud and insistent. Harley glanced in his side mirror. "Wonder what that's all about?"

"No clue." Gabe tensed, as did Mac. His expression said they were thinking the same thing. They needed to fly under the radar until Ben could pick them up.

"How far did you say that diner is?" Mac asked.

"We're about twenty minutes from Francine's Truck Stop," Harley said with an enthusiastic grin. "Best peach pie on the Front Range."

"Sounds wonderful," Mac said.

Gabe turned to the driver. "We sure appreciate this."

"No problem. I'm heading home, and Francine's is on the way." He leaned forward and looked at Gabe. "You all live around here?"

"We got in from Phoenix on Friday for the renaissance festival," Gabe said. "We spent the night at a friend's rental, and our minivan decided to breathe its last when we went to leave."

Mac was reminded of Agency training as Gabe replied. Keep the story as close to the truth as possible. It's easier to remember the truth than a lie.

"That's a shame. Mighty dangerous to be walking this road in the dark." Harley turned on the radio, and the soft crooning of a country-western song wrapped itself around them.

Winston let out a soulful sound in response, and Harley burst out laughing. "I see your dog likes country music."

"Apparently so," Mac said with a chuckle. She held the animal close and stared out the window as the night flowed past them.

The neon lights of Francine's Truck Stop came into view fifteen minutes later, just as Harley promised.

"There it is. Now you tell Fran that Harley sent you, and she'll give you a discount." He signaled and pulled into the wide drive of the truck stop.

"Thanks, Harley. You really saved the day," Mac said.

"Aw." Harley grinned. "Happy to help. Now you two be safe."

"We will," Gabe said. He opened the door of the truck and jumped down. "Come, Winston."

The bulldog eagerly jumped into Gabe's arms.

Gabe turned to Mac. "Need help?"

"I've got it," she said.

"Mac," he murmured with a smile for Harley. "A fella is supposed to assist his wife."

"Oh!" She took Gabe's hand. "Of course."

Once she stepped to the ground, Gabe put an arm around her shoulder, and together they waved at Harley as the friendly trucker pulled away. Just like they were a real couple. A normal couple.

While a part of her savored Gabe's touch, Mac nearly laughed aloud at the thought of her ever fitting into the mold of normal. She released a sigh of regret. Gabe deserved so much more than she and her emotional baggage could offer him.

When the vehicle was out of sight, Mac gave Gabe an awkward smile. "Sorry about that. I nearly messed things up."

"No problem." He pulled the burner phone from his back pocket. "Why don't you go in and grab yourself a coffee? I'll wait out here with Winston and try Ben again."

"Gabe, your arm," Mac said.

"What?"

"It's bleeding."

Gabe glanced down at his right arm. "Superficial. I ran into a branch in the woods."

She handed him her messenger bag. "I put a small first-aid kit in there."

"Mac, I'm fine."

"Take it." She shoved the bag at him and headed into the restaurant with slow steps.

Mac scanned the room, silently taking in every

single face. The couple seated at the window, laughing. The gray-haired guy in the corner with his back to her. She pulled the minivan keys from her pocket and purposely dropped them to the ground so she could get a look at him. The guy in the corner eyed her curiously before returning to his book. Nothing concerning about him.

"How can I help you, sweetie?" the woman at the counter asked.

"Two black coffees, a water and…" She glanced at the glass pastry case. The assortment of baked goods reminded her that she hadn't eaten. But her stomach was so knotted up, she didn't think she could eat anything right now. "And two muffins."

"What kind? We have blueberry, oat, banana and cinnamon-raisin."

"Banana, please." She remembered that Gabe once brought her banana bread he'd made. How odd that she should recall that right now. It had been an autumn day, and they hadn't seen each other in weeks while on separate assignments. She was only going to be home for the weekend. Saturday morning, he brought her the newspaper and banana bread. They'd walked over to Cheesman Park, read the paper and talked.

A smile lit her face at the memory.

"Is your husband okay out there?"

"What?" Mac blinked.

The woman nodded toward the door, where Gabe and Winston sat outside on a bench.

Her husband. "Oh, yes. He's fine. Our van broke down, and a trucker gave us a lift. He doesn't want to leave the dog alone."

"I don't blame him. Animals are like our children, aren't they?" She kept talking as she filled the cups with coffee from a carafe. "You two have any kids?"

"Kids?" Mac shook her head. "No. No, we don't."

The woman put lids on the cups and placed them in a carrier. She slid a white pastry bag across the counter. "Here you go."

"What do I owe you?"

"On the house. You look like you've had a tough night." She offered a gentle smile. "I remember what it was like to be young and just starting out. If it's not the car, it's the washing machine breaking down." She chuckled. "But trust me. If you can make it through the hard times, the good times will be all the sweeter."

Mac mused on her words as she pushed open the door. What would it be like to have a normal life and be married to someone like Gabe? A solid rock. Dependable. A man who loved the Lord.

She couldn't imagine a regular life and was afraid even to consider it. That was for other people, not her. Besides, guys like Gabe would want a family. She hadn't allowed herself to go down that road. It was far too terrifying.

Winston was her family.

Before the door had closed behind her, Gabe was at her side, taking the coffee tray. "Let me help you."

"Um, thanks." She met his gaze. Okay, what had changed since his almost hostile comments at the house?

"Everything look good in there?" he asked.

"Yes. Nothing out of the ordinary." She glanced around at the parking area.

Gabe placed the coffee carrier on the bench. "Quiet out here, too."

"But he's out there, isn't he?" Mac stared into the darkness. There was a shooter who wouldn't stop until she was dead. How long until he hit his target?

"Think positive. We're alive."

"What about the house?" Mac asked. "What's Addy going to say when she finds out it was shot up?"

"Avery," he said. "It's Avery. And I'm sure insurance will cover it." Gabe looked at the white sack. "What's in the bag?" She handed it to him.

"Your reward for carrying me through the woods."

He peeked inside, and his eyebrows lifted. "Nice. I should do chivalrous things more often."

Mac smiled slightly at his enthusiasm, though she remained confused at his change in attitude.

Gabe nodded toward the bench. "Have a seat.

Ben didn't pick up. I left him a message, but he hasn't returned my call yet."

"I'd rather stand."

"Are you hurting?" He leveled her with a gaze that held so much concern that she had to tell him the truth.

"Yes."

"I'm sorry."

"As you said. We're alive." She took a coffee from the carrier and removed the lid. The strong aroma of beans perked her up. "I still can't believe you carried me down that trail."

"You probably weigh less than Winston."

At the sound of his name, the bulldog perked up, looking back and forth between her and Gabe.

Gabe bit into a muffin. "Whoa, this is good. Want the other one?"

"No, thank you. Interestingly enough, while facing death gives you an appetite, it does the opposite for me." She looked around for her messenger bag and grabbed it off the end of the bench.

Digging inside the bag, Mac found Winston's small collapsible bowl. She opened a plastic zip bag and poured kibble into the bowl. The dog wasted no time chowing down.

"Is there anything you don't have in that bag?" Gabe asked, his gaze watchful and cautious again.

Mac looked out into the night once more. She took a long breath and released it. "Answers. I don't have answers."

* * *

"Ben." Gabe stood and paced in front of the bench as he held the phone to his ear. "Finally. Where are you? I was getting concerned."

"Right outside of Bluebell. Sorry it's taken me so long to get back to you. Between the car-rental issue and returning calls to my sources, the day is shot."

"As long as you're okay."

"I'm fine, and I've got intelligence regarding some of those leads."

Gabe moved out of Mac's earshot. "Great. And, um, what about that other thing I asked you to look into? Anything?"

"I've got contacts in the intelligence community with top-secret access checking on Mackenzie, but so far, everything has come back clean."

Relief caught him right between the eyes. Gabe sent up a silent prayer of thanks. He was ashamed of doubting her. Yet, his training told him that thoroughly investigating every single person attached to the mission in Toronto was procedure.

"Thanks, Ben," he said.

"Don't thank me. All that means is I haven't found evidence that she is involved. I haven't proven she's innocent."

"I get it."

"Good. Because you've still got to figure out how you're going to explain withholding information to Mackenzie. She won't be pleased, and

I don't want to be around when a woman with a Glock is annoyed."

"I'll handle Mac." He paused, glancing around to be sure he hadn't been overheard. "What about Morrow?"

"I haven't found anything the Agency wouldn't have uncovered. No activity on credit cards in eight weeks. I'll keep digging."

"Thanks."

"I'll be at Avery's in about ten minutes," Ben continued.

"We aren't at the house. We're at Francine's Truck Stop. It's on I-25, just north of Bluebell."

"Why?"

"Our shooter friend stopped by."

"Then it's good that I found a safe house." Ben paused. "I take it you and Mackenzie are okay, or you would have led with that info."

"Yeah. More or less." If *okay* meant he'd held off a shooter, all the while paranoid that the woman he was protecting could be the enemy. Then he was okay.

"Stay that way," Ben said. "I'll see you in about twenty minutes."

"Thanks, Ben." He disconnected, walked back to the bench and sank into it, emotionally exhausted.

Mac looked up at him. "Is he okay?"

"Yeah. He's been following leads on Masterson and Ribinoff. He'll be here in about twenty minutes."

"Thanks." She nodded over her shoulder. "There's a small convenience store on the other side of the diner. I'm going to go check out their amenities. We left everything but my messenger bag at your fiancée's house and I could at least use a clean T-shirt."

She's not my fiancée, Gabe mentally shot back.

"Take Winston with you, would you?" he said instead. "Flash your badge if anyone has dog issues."

"Okay." When Mac's gaze met his, Gabe grimaced. They'd been on the road since Friday, and he hadn't done anything to ease the bone weariness or pain he saw on her face. Guilt ate at him. Guilt for having doubted her loyalty even for a second and for not finding out who'd put her in this position.

"It'll get better, Mac," he said.

"Will it? It seems all we're doing is running, and we're only barely a step ahead of whoever is trying to kill me. We're trained government agents. We should be ahead of this situation."

"Tomorrow will be better. Ben said he has information."

"I hope you're right," Mac said. "Because so far, every day has only provided more obstacles and more questions."

Gabe sat down on the bench to finish his coffee as she headed to the convenience store. Yeah, he hoped he was right, too.

A few minutes after Mac and Winston returned, a dark sedan pulled into the parking lot and flashed its headlights at them.

"That's him," Gabe said.

Mac stood slowly and slipped the messenger bag over her head.

"Need any help?"

She gave a weary shake of her head. "I'm fine."

He ignored her refusal and grabbed her plastic shopping bag, then opened the back door of the sedan.

"Thanks for coming, Ben," Mac said as she slipped into the vehicle. "Come, Winston." The dog crawled over her and settled on the seat by her side.

"All three of you look exhausted," Ben said. "Sorry things went south. I got here as fast as I could."

"We're alive," Gabe said. "Everything else is gravy."

"So this is gravy?" Mac murmured to herself.

"What's the status of the house?" Ben asked.

"A few windows damaged, and a couple of bullet holes," Gabe said. "But relatively intact."

"I'm sure Avery will be glad to hear that."

"Don't remind me. I'll need to take care of that eventually."

"I'll want to go back and retrieve my duffle

and suitcase when it's daylight," Ben said. "But for now, I've found a cabin."

"A real cabin or another *Architectural Digest* layout?" Mac asked.

Ben laughed. "A real log cabin. In fact, the place is vintage seventies era."

The drive was silent, the rhythmic sounds of the road nearly lulling Gabe to sleep, until Ben tapped his arm and pointed to the back seat. When Gabe looked over his shoulder, both Mac and Winston were asleep. The dog was snoring lightly.

"It's been a long, four-day weekend," Gabe said quietly.

A few minutes later, Ben pulled into a gravel drive leading to a simple A-frame log cabin. "This is it. There's a man-made lake behind the house, lots of shade trees around the lake and about a mile of pastureland. No one is going to sneak up on us."

"How did you get this place?" Gabe asked.

"I called a vacation-rental company. They weren't going to let me have it without checking references. But the owner has a soft spot for newlyweds. I'm officially on my honeymoon."

"That works."

"Are we home?" Mac yawned and got out of the car.

Gabe's gaze followed hers as she peered at the A-frame log home. The front featured a wrap-around porch illuminated by two hanging bronze lanterns. Clay pots filled with red geraniums flanked the front door.

"Now this is a cabin," she finally said.

"Yeah," Gabe said. "I wouldn't mind retiring to a place like this. A little fishing and no people."

"You'd never survive without people," Mac said.

"She's not wrong," Ben added.

He shrugged. If being social was a flaw, he could live with it. Far better to take chances than to live a life in fear of getting close to people. If he could only convince Mac of that.

"Being social has its advantages when it comes to information gathering," Gabe finally said. "And speaking of being social. How many bedrooms?"

"Three. Two on the first floor and the entire second floor is a bedroom and office."

"Score," Gabe said to his brother.

"I called earlier and asked them to stock the place with basics so we won't have to drive into Bluebell," Ben said.

As they stepped toward the door, Gabe turned to Mac, but she held up a hand. "I know. I know. Wait here, while you and Ben do a sweep of the cabin. I'm too tired and sore to argue."

"Sorry," he returned. "I know it's been a tough day."

"For all of us," she said.

"Nice place, right?" Ben asked him as they moved through the cabin.

"Yeah. It is," Gabe said. "Functional. Not fancy. Like me."

"All clear," Ben called to Mac. He turned to Gabe. "I'm going to get some stuff from the rental car."

Winston followed Mac inside, sniffing the room with interest.

"What do you think?" Gabe asked her.

Mac stood in the center of the living area and glanced around. "Nice." She moved past the island separating the living area and the kitchen to a scarred oak table and eased into a chair.

"You okay?" he asked.

"Uh-huh." She rolled up her left pant leg, revealing the pink scar that ran down her calf. "Sometimes the leg needs a good massage."

Gabe stared at the evidence of her trauma in Toronto. Shame swept over him as the depth of her injury became real. Once again, he chastised himself for giving credence to the idea that she was involved in the bank job. If not by virtue of her moral character, surely the injury she'd suffered and continued to endure was evidence that she was innocent. In reality, he knew they'd need much more than her injury to clear her name.

"Ouch," Gabe murmured.

"My scar?" She shot him a weak smile as she rubbed the muscle. "It's so much better than it was."

"Are you in pain?"

"Yes, but it's the mosquito bites that have gotten the best of me." She glanced at the wrought-iron rooster clock on the wall. "Would you mind if I took a quick shower before we talk with Ben? I want to clean up and get some cortisone cream on the bites. The itching is overwhelming."

"You don't need to ask." He glanced around the compact kitchen and spotted a drip coffee maker. "Take your time. I'll make some coffee."

A few minutes later, Ben came into the kitchen with a paper shopping bag in his hand. "I'm going to do a quick check of the perimeter and set up cameras on the driveway and back door."

"You bought cameras?"

"I picked them up for Avery's place while I was in Denver. A little late, but they'll come in handy here."

"Good thinking."

Gabe opened the cupboards and found coffee and filters. He had the electric coffee maker gurgling within minutes. When the carafe had spit out the last drops of brew, he poured himself a cup and pulled out a chair.

"That smells good," Ben said from behind him.

"You're fast," Gabe replied. He sat down and took a cautious sip of the hot beverage. "Cameras set up?"

Ben nodded. "Yeah. The app is downloading to my phone." He glanced around. "Where's Mackenzie?"

Gabe looked past the living room to the hallway. "Taking a shower. You want to tell me what you found out about the money?"

"I had a friend check the paperwork on the account that was opened in her name eight weeks ago. Someone obtained a copy of her driver's license and other documentation to open it. I can't get information on the offshore account that wired the money into this new one."

"What about her other financial assets?"

"Everything is legit. She has a hefty inheritance and hasn't touched any of it in years. In fact—"

"Why didn't you just ask me about my finances? Why go behind my back? I have nothing to hide," Mac said.

Gabe's head jerked back when he realized Mac was standing in the entrance to the kitchen. She wore a clean T-shirt and sweatpants with the Francine's Truck Stop logo on them. Her damp blond hair had been combed back, and a red flush of anger brightened her face. She turned to Ben with steady, almost dangerous eyes.

"Would you take Winston for a walk, please? Gabe and I need to talk."

"Yeah, sure." Ben backed out of the room with a pitying glance at Gabe.

When the front door closed, Mac pinned him with her gaze as she leaned against the wall.

"After the death of my parents, I was the sole beneficiary of a substantial life-insurance policy and their modest estate. The government provided a generous settlement amount as well. Todd Shipman oversaw the funds until I turned twenty-one."

She sat down in a chair and folded her hands. Gabe swallowed, but it failed to help his dry mouth. He had never seen this scary calm behavior in Mac, and it rattled him.

"When I joined the Agency, twelve years ago, I withdrew a healthy amount of my inheritance and placed a portion of it in a floor safe in my condo. The rest of that withdrawal is in a safe-deposit box with my passport, in case I ever need untraceable funds. I emptied the safe before I left Denver for Phoenix." She looked at him. "The remainder of that withdrawal remains in my safe-deposit box. You never know when you'll need to disappear. Right?"

The insinuation was clear. He'd better come up with a good response or, as she promised on Friday, Mackenzie Sharp would be in the wind.

"Ben ran your financials at my request. Everything came back clear. If you were in my position, wouldn't you have done the same?"

"I'm not sure I understand the question." She tilted her head and looked at him. "At what point did you decide you couldn't trust me?"

Touché. She was right, and he'd feel the same way. Gabe took a deep breath, knowing that he was about to jump without a safety net.

"I received information this morning that I was

obligated to follow up on. Before he was shot, Wade Masterson told me that he was the guy in the black pickup in Albuquerque and was following us in the Colorado Renaissance Festival parking area. The implication was that he worked for Morrow in some capacity related to the bank job. I didn't get the details before he was shot. But he did tell me that Morrow told him that you had the missing bank-job money."

Mac's eyes rounded and she released a quick breath. "You withheld information from me. Again. I thought we had a deal." She paused. "You told me I had to trust someone. I chose you."

Gabe's gut burned at her words. Yeah, he did. He'd promised her they were partners. Now, when a shadow of doubt was presented, he'd become judge and jury and convicted her.

"I'm sorry, Mac. I was following protocol." Silly as it was, protocol was his only excuse.

"We're off-book. There is no protocol, except trust."

Silence maintained a tense standoff between them as the rooster clock ticked off the seconds.

"Everything okay?" Ben approached the kitchen island.

"Getting there," Gabe said.

Mac frowned, communicating that she didn't agree.

"Did Gabe update you?" Ben asked.

"Yes, but there's so much to unpack, I don't know where to start."

His brother reached for the coffee carafe and poured a cup before sitting down at the table. "Let's start unpacking," Ben said.

"Why was Wade Masterson trying to kill me?" she asked.

"If Masterson was telling the truth, it's someone else who wants you dead," Gabe said. "Masterson was working with Ribinoff. They were tracking us to locate the missing money from the bank job, not kill you."

Mac scowled. "Why would they, or Liz, for that matter, think I had the money?"

"Morrow told them you double-crossed her and took it."

She nearly jumped up from her chair at that. "Liz? Liz told them that?"

A play of expressions raced across Mac's face, until her eyes rounded with understanding and she met his gaze.

"Masterson and Ribinoff thought I was in on the bank job? They were working with Liz? He followed me, hoping I'd lead him to the money?"

Gabe nodded.

Mac opened her mouth and closed it, looking as stunned now as he was in the alley. "Is Liz alive?" she asked.

"Masterson believed she died on the pier," Gabe said. He didn't add that the man also believed Mac was responsible. Though he would certainly pay the price for the omission, right now, there was no point heaping more coals upon her head. She had enough information to digest.

"And do we have any idea who shot Masterson?" she asked.

"I think we should look into the guard, James Smith," Ben replied. "We may never get a match on the lion tattoo. It's the identifying symbol for several criminal groups. I checked, and Smith's background shows no criminal record. It would have to be clean to get him hired as a bank guard."

"I'm still trying to wrap my head around the idea that Liz was actually involved in the bank job. Is she connected to Smith somehow?" Mac asked.

"A very good question," his brother said. "My intelligence sources tell me that all of them, Smith, Ribinoff and Masterson, aged out of foster care. If Liz did grow up in the system, as she accidentally revealed to you, it's very likely all of their paths crossed hers. My guess would be that she recruited them."

Gabe considered his brother's theory for a moment. It made sense, but they couldn't actually prove any of it.

Unless they got Ribinoff to talk.

"I don't understand," Mac said. "Why didn't the Agency or Canadian law enforcement pick up on this?"

"Why would they?" Gabe responded immediately. "The bank guard is who they were looking at. Masterson and Ribinoff, and even Morrow, weren't on their radar. There was no reason for law enforcement to dig into the foster-care angle. Ben is the first one to connect the dots that no one even noticed until today. So it wouldn't have come up on a background check."

Once again, confusion had Mac frowning. Gabe related. They had plenty of information but not enough answers. He'd already come up with many of the same questions Mac had.

"What are you thinking?" he asked Mac.

"If the foster-care connection is valid, who altered Liz's file?"

"Someone with admin access," Ben said.

"Like Blake Calder." Mac looked to Gabe and he nodded.

"Recently transferred to the Denver field office. He's the number-two guy under Shipman. He'd have admin access." Gabe gave a slow shake of his head. "That would explain how the shooter found us at Avery's house. The laptop Calder gave us."

"That I can agree with," Mac said. "The rest... I'm not so sure. I mean, think about it. The Agency tracks every access on the intranet. They require regular polygraphs and annual investigations. How did he pull off a plan this big?"

"No intelligence-gathering network is perfect," Ben said. "Once again, I'm speculating. I believe that whoever is involved is playing a long game, requiring patience." He paused and sipped his coffee. "Every instance of access into files would have been a small tweak, so no one noticed. They built their game one move at a time over a long period of time, without calling attention to themselves."

One piece at a time. Gabe nodded. Yeah, it would require months of focused patience with an eye on the prize. Twenty million dollars.

"It would be helpful if I could remember where I've seen Calder before." Mac stood, moved to the island and poured coffee into a cup.

"You could have seen him anywhere." Gabe shrugged. "While he's new to Denver, Shipman told me he's had assignments in several field offices in the States and abroad."

Calder had experience, but he was a benign enough character to move anonymously on a daily basis. Plus, he was high enough in the food chain to have the access needed to pull off the heist undetected.

Mac nodded, her gaze directed out the window, apparently thinking. "So, how is Ribinoff connected?"

"If Ben's theory is correct, then it makes sense that Ribinoff and Masterson were following someone's instructions. Masterson admitted that Ribinoff was his inside guy," Gabe said.

"Ribinoff just happened to get a job with the Agency?" She shot him a doubtful look.

"We can't prove anything yet," Ben said. "I'd theorize that someone in authority paved the way for Ribinoff to be hired."

Calder again, Gabe surmised.

"Who killed Masterson?" Mac asked.

"Once again, our shooter strikes," Ben said. "My money is still on James Smith."

"Do you think Liz was involved with the bank job from the start?" Mac asked.

Ben cocked his head and gave a quick shrug. "We can't prove anything, but it sure smells like both Morrow and Calder were the masterminds."

"And do you think Liz faked her death on the pier?"

"That's the twenty-million-dollar question," Ben said.

Mac looked from Ben to Gabe, her expression bleak, and he knew what she was thinking.

All this time, she'd carried the guilt of the death of her team member and the asset. If they could find Morrow and prove she was involved, Mac could be released from her self-inflicted prison.

Gabe turned to his brother. "If Morrow masterminded the bank job and faked her own death, why didn't she just walk away? Disappear?" He raised his palms in question. "I keep circling back to that."

"Because Mackenzie is a loose end." Ben narrowed his eyes. "She's the only person besides Calder who can connect Liz to the foster-care system and to Smith, Ribinoff and Masterson."

"Do you think that's it?" Mac asked.

"Yes," Ben returned. "It may not seem like much, but you can connect the dots. You just didn't know it."

Mac's eyes widened. "Does that mean Liz is alive?"

Once again, Gabe's brother shrugged. "We don't have enough information to make that determination."

"He's right," Gabe said. "There are still too many variables."

"Shouldn't we get this intel to your boss?" Ben asked.

"Not yet," Mac said. "We don't have proof of anything."

"What about Ribinoff?" Gabe turned to Ben. "What did you find out?"

"I have his last known address. Tomorrow morning, we should stake it out."

"We need Ribinoff," Gabe said. "I'm sure we can get him to talk if we offer him a deal."

"We're running an unauthorized operation here. We don't have the authority to offer anything," Mac argued. Once again, her voice was chilly.

"He doesn't know that," Gabe said.

Ben stood and reached into the shopping bag on the table and pulled out two packages of burner phones. "Next order of business. You two need to destroy any phones you have. I picked up a couple of new burners for you."

"Thanks." Gabe looked at the rooster clock. "What time are we leaving in the morning?"

"Sunrise is five forty-five a.m.," Ben said. "I'd like to stop at Avery's to grab my stuff, and arrive in Denver before then."

Gabe groaned.

"Could we find my cane?"

"If you bring that handy flashlight of yours we can," Gabe said. "I mean, since my brother's plan has us out the door in the middle of the night."

Ben laughed at his words and stood. "I'm taking a shower. And I'll take the first watch." He offered a short salute. "Night, all."

A flash of pain crossed Mac's face as she slowly got up as well. Without looking at him, she went to the counter and poured herself more coffee. Now was the time to reach out to her and hope that she could see things from his side of the table.

"I'm sorry, Mac," Gabe said. "I hope you'll forgive me."

"Oh, I forgive you. I don't know where we stand with the whole trust thing, though." She turned. "Tell me. Did you really believe I had gone rogue?"

"When that shooter showed up at the house, I knew I had to make a decision." He met her gaze. "Wade Masterson's words rang in my head. He said you had the money. I had to decide if I believed you were part of the plot. Had you taken the money from Morrow as he was convinced?"

"And?"

"I went with what my heart and my head were telling me. There was no way the Mackenzie Sharp I knew could be involved. Period. Still, it was in your best interest that we find out how you'd been implicated. Ben's investigative work provided paper evidence that someone else opened that offshore account. Your financials show that you've had a substantial portfolio for some time. While that isn't proof for the Agency that you weren't involved, it's enough for me."

She stared at him with enough concentration to start a small fire. Would his admission end the tension between them?

"Why didn't you leave me in Phoenix?" Gabe took a deep breath. "Leave me on the ground when the SUV exploded? You weren't sure you could trust me. But you went with your gut and gave me a chance. It's the same thing."

"Is it?" She offered a curt nod and picked up her cup. "Good night, Denton."

Denton.

They were back to square one. For the fourth or fifth time. Gabe ran a hand over his face and prayed for patience.

NINE

"This is Ribinoff's place?" Mac asked.

Ben nodded as he drove past the apartment complex.

Mac grimaced. Fiesta Apartments in the light of a Tuesday dawn in Denver was nothing to celebrate.

Two floors of units and every apartment door had a view of the parking area. Streetlamps at the corners of the building cast more shadows than light. Not even the arrival of daylight in another thirty minutes could alter the drab appearance of the apartment complex.

"I'm depressed just looking at it," Mac said.

"Great place to stay if you want to keep a low profile," Ben said.

"Which apartment is his?" Mac asked. Once again, she directed her questions and comments to Ben. It was early. She hadn't had coffee, and cranky had settled on her like a scratchy sweater. While she'd forgiven Gabe, she wasn't ready to let him off the hook for his acute episode of protocol yesterday.

"Last apartment on the right, first floor," Ben said.

Mac said a silent thank-you. Her leg wasn't prepared to handle stairs yet, and her pride wouldn't allow her to admit that fact.

Gabe pulled out his binoculars. "The lights are on. All of them."

"Maybe he's a morning person," his brother said.

"This isn't morning," Gabe groused. "But let's park the car and find out."

"You say that like there's a place to park." Ben glanced around the dark street.

"The alley looks good," Mac said. "It's too early for trash collection."

"Good idea." Ben eased the vehicle into the alley.

"All clear," Mac said as she exited the car.

Gabe approached the door to Ribinoff's apartment first, weapon raised, while Ben positioned himself on the other side of the door. Mac remained in the parking area, eyes on the apartment.

Suddenly, the door burst open, slamming against the building's exterior wall with a reverberating bang. A tall man ran out, knocking Gabe to the ground. Head down, face hidden by a hoodie, the light from the streetlamps reflecting off the 9 mm in his right hand.

"He's got a weapon," Ben yelled.

Mac's cane clattered to the ground as she hit the pavement behind a parked car and withdrew her Glock from the ankle holster. Tension kept her fingers tightly gripping her weapon.

"In pursuit." Ben raced through the parking lot after the fleeing man.

Gabe scrambled to his feet and whipped around. "Mac?" His eyes connected with hers.

"I'm okay."

"Are you carrying?"

"Yes." She held up the Glock.

"Can you cover the apartment while I cover Ben?"

"Go. Go. I can handle this." Mac inched to a half-sitting position and eyed the perimeter. The door to the apartment was open. There was no movement inside. With a hand on the car's bumper, she struggled to stand, searching for her cane.

Minutes later, Ben and Gabe returned.

"Lost him," Ben panted.

Gabe stood hunched over, hands on knees, catching his breath. "I'm too old for this. I want a nice cushy office job."

"Like managing partner of Denton Security and Investigations, perhaps?" Ben asked.

Gabe only glared at his brother.

"Was it Ribinoff?" Mac asked.

"No way," Gabe said. "The guy who ran out of that apartment was tall and muscular. He fits the physical profile of the Toronto shooter. James Smith."

Mac swallowed hard at the words. If he'd seen her, would he have turned that 9 mm on her?

"You're looking pale, Mac. You okay?" Gabe asked.

"Fine. What about you? He knocked you down."

"Yeah, he did." Gabe nodded and rubbed his back. "And I'll be feeling that tomorrow."

"The door is still open," Mac said. She motioned toward the apartment building.

Gabe followed her gaze. "That's not good."

"It's also not good that lights are coming on all over the complex," Ben said.

The three of them cautiously approached the open door, with Mac taking up the rear.

Gabe entered first. "Clear," he called out from the living room.

"Any sign of your tech?" Ben asked.

"Not yet," Gabe said. "Kitchen is clear."

Mac entered the first bedroom, weapon ready. The bed was rumpled but empty. He'd been here. She pulled open the closet door using the edge of her T-shirt and then checked under the bed.

Pausing, Mac backtracked to get a better look under the bed. Was that a dust bunny? Left leg awkwardly extended, she knelt on her right knee. A cell phone? She pulled a tissue out of her pocket and grabbed the phone.

"Bedroom is clear," she called out.

In the hallway, Gabe and Ben had positioned themselves outside another door. Gabe nodded, and Ben pushed open the door to what looked like an office. Mac followed behind cautiously as they entered the room.

A crumpled body lay next to the desk.

Though high-end electronics and computer equipment fought for space on the desk, nothing seemed amiss in the room.

Except Ribinoff.

Both Ben and Gabe knelt next to the body.

"Poor kid." Hands trembling, Mac looked away. Another death and for what end? Money?

"He's still warm," Ben said. "Single GS to the back of the head. He probably didn't even see it coming."

"The kid didn't deserve this." Gabe shook his head and ran a hand over his face, visibly shaken. "Some days, I hate my job."

"Someone is tying up loose ends," Ben said. "We need to find them before they find Mackenzie."

"Let's get out of here," Mac said. "We can make an anonymous 911 call in the car."

The drive back to Bluebell was solemn. Mac wrestled with her thoughts. Her job had been about intelligence gathering up to now. Ever since Toronto, everything had changed.

The only way to stop the domino of events was to get ahead of the situation. Then maybe no one else would die. She pulled the cell phone wrapped in tissue from her pocket and stared at it for minutes. Maybe there was something here that would help.

When Ben turned into the gravel drive of the A-frame cabin and parked the car, Mac cleared her throat. "I have Ribinoff's cell phone. It was under his bed."

Gabe turned in his seat to look at her, his expression appalled. "You took the cell phone?"

"I borrowed it. It's not like he'll need it." She looked at him, annoyed. "Seriously, Gabe? We're running blind here. We don't have access to the Agency resources and we're trying to stay one step ahead of some very bad people. This might tip the odds in our favor."

"I get that. What I don't get is why you're just saying something now."

"Because she knew you'd object to removing something from the scene," Ben said. "Let's take it inside. I have gloves."

"So I like to follow protocol," Gabe grumbled as they entered the cabin and went into the kitchen. "Some people find that quality admirable."

Mac ignored him. "There's a voice mail on this phone." She sat at the kitchen table and donned the gloves Ben gave her. Then she pressed the voice-mail button.

"You've called in sick for the next few days,

Ezra," a voice rang out. *"I've taken care of everything. Just stay low until I call back. I'm arranging your flight."*

"That's Calder," Gabe said.

Mac shivered. "Calder, again. And I still can't figure out why that guy seems so familiar. Maybe he was in Toronto."

"Was he on the flight you and Morrow took to Toronto?" Gabe asked.

"We flew commercial. It's possible, but I didn't notice him in the boarding area."

"Slow it down, Mackenzie," Ben said. "Small memories can trigger big memories. You remembered that tattoo. You can remember this."

She nodded. Ben was right—she'd pushed everything from the last eight weeks into a drawer that she'd locked away. Opening it up and carefully sorting through each memory could yield valuable information again. Though it came with risks, she was willing to try.

"Give us a play-by-play of the day you left for Toronto."

"I took Winston to the boarding place."

Mac closed her eyes for a moment and concentrated, but all she could hear was the accelerated thump of her heart pounding in her head. She took a deep breath and, using the biofeedback techniques she'd learned long ago to ease anxiety, slowed her breathing and heart rate.

"When I got home, I called a ride-share service

to get to the airport. Which is a good thing, or my car would still be in long-term parking."

"You and Morrow didn't go to the airport together?" Ben asked.

"No. Never. She always declined the offer to carpool."

Mac was silent for a moment, rubbing the bridge of her nose. "Airport departures." *One by one, the driver had passed each airline drop-off point before pulling to the curb in front of mine.*

She released a small gasp as the memory materialized. "That's it!" Mac worked to control the trembling of her voice. "That's where I saw Calder. At airport departures. My ride-share dropped me off, and I stood at the curb, adding the tip to my ride. I looked up and saw Liz arrive farther down." She nodded. "Calder exited the same vehicle as Liz and handed her a suitcase from the trunk. Then he kissed her. It was an intimate kiss."

"You saw his face?"

"Only in profile. But I'm certain it was him. Absolutely certain."

"So Calder has…or had a relationship with Morrow," Gabe said. "Who is giving the kill orders?"

"Good question," Ben said.

"Do you think Shipman knows Calder is the mole?" Mac asked.

"I don't think so. He trusted Calder to meet us," Gabe said.

"We should call Shipman," Mac insisted.

"No," Ben said. "You're already a liability to Calder. If he somehow intercepts a phone call and finds out that you can ID him with Morrow, who knows what he might do."

"But Shipman needs our intel." Withholding info from each other had been getting them nowhere, and Mac wasn't going to keep Shipman out of the loop any longer. "In person. Tonight. After dark."

"You're going to Shipman's house?" Gabe looked at her. "Is that wise?"

"Wisdom isn't part of the equation. Expedience is, if we're going to stop them," she said. "I might not agree with how this situation is being handled by the Agency, but I still trust Shipman."

"Okay. Then we're going to talk to him," he said. "Together."

"Once again, you don't trust me?" Mac sighed and gave a slow shake of her head.

"I don't trust the shooter who wants you dead."

"He's right, Mackenzie," Ben said. "You have to take backup with you. I'll stay here with Winston."

"Fine," she said. "We leave at midnight."

"Because getting sleep at night would be out of the question," Gabe muttered. Winston trotted into the kitchen and put his head on Gabe's lap.

Mac couldn't help but notice how her dog was becoming more and more attached to Gabe.

"The first thing I'm going to do when this is over is find some good sushi and then sleep for a week." Gabe looked at Winston. "What are you going to do, buddy?"

The dog whined and flopped down on the floor.

Mac stood and looked from the dog to the man. Winston was going to miss Gabe when this was over. She empathized with her dog. Despite his trust missteps, she feared she would feel the same way.

She offered Gabe a nod. "I'll see you at midnight."

"Have you thought about what we're going to do once we get there?" Gabe asked. He glanced at Mac in the passenger seat. She'd been less antagonistic since they'd left Bluebell. And silent for the most part, which he chose to interpret as a step toward reconciliation of their friendship.

"Yes," she answered. "I'll text him using my new burner."

Gabe turned into the Cherry Creek neighborhood and noted the neighborhood-watch and security signs.

"This is where he lives now?" Mac asked.

"Yeah. He's leasing a place."

"Leasing in a nice neighborhood. Old money mixed with new money," she observed.

"Pretty much," Gabe said. "I haven't been to

his home since he and Mary moved." He handed her his phone. "Directions are on here."

"Keep going straight." Mac leaned forward in her seat, eyeing the street signs. "Slow down."

"Sorry."

"Turn left into the next cul-de-sac." She pointed as he turned. "That's it, the second house on the right."

Gabe parked in front of the house and got out. He assessed the neighborhood as he stood in the street. While not a mansion, the Shipmans' two-story brick Tudor home indicated affluence. He wouldn't be surprised if there were hidden cameras beneath the eaves. Shipman could very well have already been alerted to their presence.

Mac sent a quick text and moved behind the shadow of a looming Douglas fir.

"He got your message." Gabe motioned toward the second floor, where lights now glowed behind the closed blinds.

"Duck, Gabe," Mac said.

"What?" He tensed and glanced around before stepping into the shadows right before the headlights of the neighborhood rent-a-cops swept past. "Thanks."

A few minutes later, the front door opened, and Todd Shipman stepped outside. His graying hair was mussed, and he wore a crisp dark dress shirt and jeans. "Mackenzie, Denton. Glad to see you both in one piece."

"Sorry to disturb you and Mrs. Shipman, sir." Gabe was already regretting Mac's midnight rendezvous plan.

"Not at all. I expected you to visit long before this." He paused. "Though I'll admit, I was surprised when the cameras went off and I saw you two in my drive." Shipman nodded toward the side yard. "Let's go around to the back. Voices carry out here."

They followed him through a fence to a backyard lush with pots overflowing with blooming flowers. A gentle light lit up a cobblestone patio that held more furniture than he had in his whole apartment.

"Please, sit." Shipman pulled out chairs at a glass-topped table. "You're safe here. Two of my neighbors are law enforcement, and another is a martial-arts instructor. I have them on speed dial." He pulled a Glock from his waistband and set it on the table. "And I still manage to qualify on the range, once a year."

Of course he did. Gabe nearly laughed aloud. This was typical Shipman. Formidable with a dry sense of humor that caught you off guard.

Mac sat down across from Gabe.

"How's your leg, Mackenzie?" Shipman asked.

"Fair to middling, sir."

"What do you two know about Ezra Ribinoff's death?" Shipman's change of topic had Gabe's head spinning.

"I…um…" Mac stuttered and turned to Gabe.

"There's no proof yet, but we believe he was working with the team that pulled the Toronto bank job," Gabe said.

"That's a shame." Shipman shook his head. "Always regrettable when one of our own is lost." He took a deep breath. "Any idea who turned him?"

"Only a theory," Gabe said. "An investigation will no doubt alert the inside person."

"Blake Calder," Shipman said with a knowing nod.

Gabe and Mac looked at each other in stunned surprise.

"I am the head of the Denver office of the Central Intelligence Agency, people. And I pride myself in staying a step ahead."

"But how did you figure out Calder?" Gabe asked.

"Found a listening device in my office today. No one else had access except Calder and my secretary. She's been with the Agency through so many presidential elections that I've lost count. Unlikely that she'd risk her pension."

"What are you going to do about Calder?" Mac asked.

"For now, I have agents watching him." He turned to Mac. "Does Elizabeth Morrow play into your theory?"

"Yes, sir." She paused and looked at Shipman

beneath the pale glow of the back porch, then glanced at Gabe.

She was hesitant to share, and Gabe didn't blame her. Shipman himself suspected Calder, which helped their case. Would he believe Morrow's involvement when they had nothing but unsubstantiated intel?

"It's possible that Liz used her past in foster care to recruit at least three of her former foster-care brothers that we know of into this plan," Mac said. "James Smith, Ezra Ribinoff and Wade Masterson."

"Masterson. The man shot in the alley, blocks from the field office," Shipman said.

"Yes, sir." Mac nodded.

"Morrow's file doesn't indicate foster care," Shipman said.

"We believe Calder altered her file and paved the way for Ribinoff's employment with the Agency," Gabe began. "Either Morrow or Calder, or both, assisted James Smith in getting the bank-guard position, and masterminded the entire robbery."

"That's an elaborate plan, and as you said, there's no evidence. At least not yet, correct?"

"Yes, sir," Mac said.

"This is day five and the Agency hasn't been able to verify Morrow is alive. In fact, except for her Agency footprints, we haven't been able to find much of anything." Shipman frowned. "Do you two have any insights?"

"Very few," Gabe said. "Ribinoff and Masterson were under the assumption that Morrow was dead. They were told that Mac was in on the robbery and took the money from Morrow."

"Mackenzie." Shipman nodded slowly as though contemplating his words. "Which explains framing her with the offshore account."

"I, um…" Mac paused. "I hope you don't think I had anything to do with that."

Shipman shook his head. "There are an inordinate number of unknown variables, Mackenzie. You are not one of them."

"Thank you, sir."

Gabe shared the audible relief he heard in Mac's voice.

"What about the shooter?"

"We think he shot Masterson and Ribinoff and has been after Mac since Toronto."

"Sounds like someone is tying up loose ends to me," Shipman said.

Exactly their thoughts. Gabe nodded. Good to know they were on the same page as Shipman.

"Any idea who the shooter is?" Shipman continued.

"Possibly James Smith, the bank guard," Mac said.

"As I recall, Calder reached out and recommended Morrow for the Toronto assignment be-

fore he was even moved to the Denver office."
Shipman was silent for a moment. "Do we have
anything on him?"

Mac pulled a plastic bag from her pocket. "Ribinoff's cell phone. Though he doesn't identify
himself, Calder is on a voice mail left yesterday.
There are multiple phone numbers that we believe
are Calder's and Morrow's."

"I'll need a warrant to obtain the phone re-
cords," Shipman said. "And I'm going to have to
do that without Calder finding out." He picked
up the plastic bag gingerly. "I don't want to know
how you obtained this, do I?"

"It was just lying around, sir," Mac said.

"I see." He looked from Mac to Gabe. "At best,
this is circumstantial evidence. However, it may
help me convince Calder to flip and talk to Homeland Security. But that won't change the fact that
there is still a shooter out there."

"Yes, sir," Gabe said.

"Why are you being targeted, Mackenzie?"
Shipman asked.

"I stumbled upon the truth about Morrow's
background without realizing how important the
information is. I know enough to raise questions
that could ultimately put Smith, Calder and, if
she's alive, Morrow behind bars."

"I'll have their passports red-flagged as a pre-
caution. They won't be able to leave the country."

Shipman frowned. "You both understand we never had this discussion."

Gabe nodded.

"Yes, sir," Mac said.

Shipman looked at Mac, his eyes filled with concern. "Mackenzie, be very careful. Whether Morrow is dead or alive, someone is trying to kill you."

"Yes, sir."

Gabe followed Mac back to the car. She was silent as she got in and fastened her seat belt.

"What are you thinking?" he asked.

"I think it's time to go after Calder."

"Shipman will handle Calder."

"Yes, I'm very familiar with the speed at which the wheels of bureaucracy move. I want to follow Calder now and see if he leads us to Liz or James Smith."

"I get that, but I won't let you use yourself as bait," he said.

She looked at him.

"No, Mac, that option is off the table."

The dogged expression in her eyes said that she hadn't agreed to anything.

Hours after the meeting with Shipman, Mac stepped into the living room, where she found Ben reading. An old-fashioned kerosene lamp sat on the table next to him. Outside, rain danced on the windows, and in the corner, Winston had sprawled on a rug, and was softly snoring.

"Mackenzie, did the storm wake you?" Ben closed the book in his lap and stood.

"No. I've been thinking about the meeting with Shipman and I couldn't sleep. Why don't I take over now? There's no use both of us being awake."

"Sure. Okay. Thanks a lot." He motioned to the lamp. "Power is out. I imagine that happens a lot here. It'll probably be back up by morning. I cracked a few windows to create a cross breeze."

Mac nodded. As Ben turned to leave, she touched his arm. "Thank you."

"For what?"

"For coming, for putting yourself on the line."

"Friends do that. Gabe would do it for me and for you, too."

"Friends," she murmured. "He doesn't seem to trust this friend."

Ben met her gaze, his eyes searching. "Haven't we already had this conversation? My brother cares for you more than a friend, which is why he tends to overreact to issues that concern you."

"I know you mean well, but is it possible you're working with old data?"

He started laughing, his eyes crinkling with amusement, just like Gabe's. "The data is current," Ben said.

Mac raised a hand and then dropped it to her side. What could she say to that?

"You know this job isn't exactly conducive to caring."

"Yeah, I get it. The job, always the job. Which is why I got out. I want a future and a family, and I want that family to come first." He paused. "Not the job. God and my family, and then my country and the job. It's the only way that works."

Mac nodded, mulling Ben's admission. She'd dared to consider a life outside of the Agency in the last few weeks. That was a huge step. Could she follow through and take a chance on the possibility that someone like her could have a family? Once again, the idea terrified her.

"Don't hurt him again. I'm not sure he could handle it a second time."

"Gabe was engaged. Clearly, he moved on," she countered.

"No. Not really. Fortunately, he figured that out before the wedding." He winked. "That's between you and me."

"Thank you, Ben. I appreciate your honesty."

He nodded and left the room.

Though her response to Ben had appeared calm, inside she was overwhelmed with confusion. She turned over his words again and again, with no idea what to do about them. She and Gabe couldn't go back.

Could they go forward?

The only sound was the clock on the wall. Mac stood at the window, staring out at the rain falling on the small lake. Each droplet created a dance of circles.

She cranked the window open a little more and inhaled the earthy scent of soil after the rain.

A chilly breeze rushed past, mixing in the smell of pine from the big tree next to the cabin.

Mac glanced at the coffeepot in the kitchen. No electricity, but she could boil water on the gas range and make tea. She carried the kerosene lamp to the kitchen table and began opening cupboards, until she found a small pot.

Staring mindlessly into the pan of water on the gas burner, she waited for the bubbles to simmer on the bottom and break the surface.

The pantry held several choices of tea bags. She chose chamomile, poured the hot water into her mug and sat down.

Her dream would be to live in a place like this. Away from people, away from threats and away from the Agency.

What did retired operatives do with the rest of their lives? It sounded like a bad pun.

"Couldn't sleep, huh?"

Mac turned around at Gabe's words. He wore a disheveled T-shirt with jeans, and his hair was totally mussed, which made him an adorable nerd. She glanced away.

"Where's Ben?"

"I relieved him." She glanced at the rooster clock. "It's four a.m. What are you doing up?"

"My internal clock is confused. From DC to Denver, to Phoenix, and back to Denver." Gabe smiled and opened a cupboard.

"What are you looking for?"

"The beans." Pulling out a silver package, he rolled back the packaging and sniffed. "Nice."

"Isn't there ground coffee? The electricity is out."

"There must be a grinder around here."

"You'll wake Ben."

Gabe frowned and opened a few more cupboards until he pulled something out. "I'm talking an old-fashioned hand grinder." He carefully measured out the beans and dumped them in the grinder. Turning the handle, he stopped periodically to evaluate the grind.

"Perfect."

"But the coffee maker doesn't work."

"If there's a kerosene lamp—" Gabe nodded toward the one flickering on the kitchen table "—then the electricity goes out regularly." He pulled out an aluminum stove-top coffeepot from the cupboard, lifted the lid and filled it with water, before adding the ground beans to the basket.

Five minutes later, the smell of fresh coffee filled the kitchen.

"Mind if I trade my tea for a cup of that?"

He laughed. "You're drinking herbal. That might be a good thing."

"Herbal tea isn't going to slow down my mind.

Things are about to blow wide open. It's like the still before a tornado. I feel it in my spirit." She looked at him again and her heart ached with concern. "I couldn't handle it if something happened to you because of me, Gabe. It would be my fault again."

"Again? You're talking about your parents?"

Mac nodded. She'd held everything inside for so long. Even from Gabe. Especially from Gabe. Now, here she was rambling and couldn't stop. "I have so much…guilt about that night."

"Stop looking back. There was nothing you could have done to prevent the bombing. Nothing."

"I snuck out of the house on a dare." She swallowed a sob, intent on her admission. "I don't deserve to be alive."

"Don't say that. You were a kid, and you know there is no causal relationship between what happened at the embassy and your youthful activity."

Mac reached for his hands as anxiety choked her. "I can't do it again. I can't handle it if someone else I care about is killed."

"You can't live your life worried that people are going to die, either. They are. This world is only a stop on the way to forever, Mac. People die. God is our only hope."

She looked down at her hands in his and pulled hers away. Now she was being foolish.

Gabe cupped her face with his palm. It would

be easy to lean into the comfort he offered, but that wouldn't be fair to him.

"Talk to me, Mac." Gabe's warm voice slid over her skin, and she shivered.

Again, she edged away from his touch. Despite their ongoing trust issues, when she looked into Gabe's eyes, she was unable to deny how much she cared. So much so, that she feared she was close to falling in love with him again.

"Ever think maybe it's time to get out?" she asked.

"Sure. All the time," he said.

"Don't tell Shipman, but if we get out of here alive, I'm thinking about turning in my resignation." *There, she'd said it. For the first time in her life, she was considering putting her past behind her to grab the possibility of a future.*

"*When.* Not *if* we get out of here alive," Gabe corrected with a frown. "And I have to tell you, Mac, you are the last person I would have ever guessed would leave the Agency."

"Things change. People change."

"I'll agree with that." He looked at her as though both confused and intrigued. "What are you going to do next?"

"I don't have a clue." She stared out the window at the lake.

What would it be like to have a normal life? Everything came down to whether or not she had the courage to find out.

TEN

Gabe checked his watch and kept his eyes on the front door of the Denver field office. Well after 5:00 p.m. on a Wednesday and yet, no Calder.

He adjusted his Bluetooth and spoke to his brother again. "Nothing yet."

"Where are you?" Ben asked.

"Mac and I are parked across the street from the parking garage in a black minivan, Texas plates," Gabe said.

"Another minivan?" Ben noted.

Gabe chuckled. "They blend in. What can I say?"

Mac turned in the passenger seat to face Gabe. "How'd you get Ben into the Agency parking garage?"

"I gave him my pass."

"You have a parking pass?" she sputtered. "I park on the street."

"I'm a VIP visitor. I have to turn it back in when I leave for DC." Gabe bit back a laugh at the expression on Mac's face.

Minutes passed until, finally, Gabe spotted a group of employees leaving the building across the street. "Here he comes."

Gabe and Mac both slid down in their seats.

"I've got my eyes on his parking stall," Ben said. "Silver BMW with vanity plates."

"Roger that," Gabe said.

"So what we're going to do is follow him and hope he leads us to Smith or Morrow?" Mac frowned.

"Do you have a better plan?" Gabe asked.

"Yes. I vote for confronting him."

"So he can disappear?" Gabe shook his head. "All we have is a bunch of theories. We need more information."

"Exiting parking garage in the BMW and turning left," Ben said minutes later. "I'm two vehicles behind in the black sedan."

"Here we go." Gabe started the minivan and turned to Mac. "Seat belt."

She buckled up and checked her mirror as he pulled into traffic. "Do you think Winston is safe at the cabin alone?"

"Ben has cameras set up. Winston is safer there than here, where he could take a stray bullet if things go south again. You can't worry about him when you're supposed to focus on keeping yourself safe."

"You're right. I know you're right. I still hate leaving him."

"Calder's parking garage is two blocks ahead, on the right," Ben said.

Gabe glanced at Mac and her expression said they were thinking the same thing. Would he lead them to Smith or possibly Morrow, if she was alive?

"Hang on a minute." Gabe narrowed his eyes and assessed the traffic in front of him. "Ben, Calder has another tail."

"You've got to be kidding me," his brother returned.

"I'm four vehicles behind you. A burgundy pickup truck pulled into traffic. He's moving fast and coming up next to you on the right. It looks like he's going to try to edge in behind Calder."

"I see him," Ben said. "I'm not going to let him in."

Gabe signaled left. "I'm diverting to a side street. You stay with Calder. No one can ID you. We can't take the chance that they'd make Mac and me. Just keep me updated on your location and I'll stay in the vicinity."

"Calder just turned into underground parking. I'm going to follow."

"What about the truck, Ben?" Gabe asked.

"He's right behind me on the entrance ramp."

The sound of shots firing echoed in Gabe's ear and had him swallowing, as adrenaline surged.

"Ben!" Jaw tight, Gabe clenched the steering wheel.

"Ben, what's going on?" Mac asked.

"It's Smith. He's got Calder pinned down inside his vehicle."

Gabe made a hard right into the next lane, jerking both him and Mac sideways.

Horns blared as he cut off a cabbie, who was now behind him.

"Come on. Come on. Come on," Gabe muttered, fist pounding on the steering wheel. He had to get to that parking garage.

"What do you want me to do?" Gabe asked his brother.

"Block the exit. Maybe we can get a twofer. Keep Calder alive for Shipman and grab Smith."

"Okay, but I'd like to keep us alive, too."

"I'm all for that," Ben said as another shot rang out.

"On my way." Gabe said a silent apology as he cut off another vehicle and turned onto the entrance ramp of the parking garage. Gripping the steering wheel, he did a quick three-point turn to block the exit.

He looked at Mac. "I know you hate to hear this, but please stay in the vehicle. Smith will pick you off like cans on a fence if you're walking down that ramp. Hide on the floor in the back in case he rams the van out of the way, and have your weapon ready."

"What about you?" she asked, her face reflecting concern.

He unfastened his seat belt and opened the door of the minivan. "I'm going to run up to the next level and assess the situation. Smith won't know I'm there."

"That's your plan?" Mac grimaced.

"I'll improvise and pray." He pulled out his weapon and eyed the ramp.

"I'll be praying, too."

His gaze met hers and he gave a nod. "Thanks." It didn't escape him that Mackenzie Sharp, who seemed to be having a crisis of faith, had offered to pray for him. He was going to be the one to pray with her, yet she'd taken the lead. Gabe nearly laughed aloud as he jumped out of the vehicle.

"Keep her safe, Lord," he murmured.

Mac got out of the minivan, removed the Glock from her ankle holster and slipped into the back. "Stay on comms, Gabe."

"Will do."

A gunshot rang out, ricocheting off the walls of the garage, its sound amplified in the cement structure.

Gabe took off running, his eyes everywhere. Thankfully, there were no civilians in sight.

The smell of exhaust and gasoline wrapped up in the heat of the day greeted him as he raced uphill to the second level of the parking garage.

"Where are you, Ben?" he panted.

"Ground floor. Section B. I've got eyes on Smith and Calder. Both are inside their vehicles."

"Does Calder have a weapon?"

"It doesn't appear that he does. He hasn't returned fire. Smith has a sniper rifle. I can see the fat barrel when he pokes it out the window."

Gabe eyed the walls for section numbers. He found section B and moved slowly to the yellow barrier rail. Looking down to the ground floor, he spotted Calder's BMW sideways against the cement wall, as if he was going to turn the vehicle around but stopped. He could see Calder on the floor of the Beemer.

Ben's rental sedan was the only thing between Calder and the pickup. The driver's door was open, and the vehicle was now minus his brother.

The pickup truck was right beneath where Gabe stood.

Where was Ben?

Gabe scanned the area, searching between vehicles until he finally spotted his brother, weapon ready, crouched down next to his rental vehicle, with a clear line of sight to both Smith and Calder.

"Look up," Gabe said softly.

Ben did. He smiled and gave a thumbs-up.

"What are you doing?" Gabe asked.

"I'm doing my best to keep Smith from killing Calder. Every time Smith opens the door of his pickup to get out, I fire. Then I move to another position. He's pinned in his truck."

Gabe tensed with anger as he recalled Masterson and Ribinoff lying in puddles of their own blood.

"I'm convinced this is the same shooter who took out Masterson and Ribinoff and nearly killed Mac and me on the train tracks," Gabe said. "It's time to shut him down."

"What do you have in mind?" Ben asked.

"I'm going jump into the flatbed. Cover me."

"No, you can't do that. Smith will nail you."

"Extended cab. I'll roll toward the window, and he won't even be able to see me from the driver's seat. While he's trying to figure out what happened, you get Calder out of his car and into the elevator."

"I won't be able to cover you, if I do that."

"Once I'm in the back of the truck, I'll be fine."

Ben was silent for a moment and he knew his brother was calculating. "Okay. I don't like it, but I don't have another plan."

Gabe looked down at the truck, gauging the distance. He climbed over the barrier and stood on the edge with one hand on the metal rail.

He looked down at Ben. "Ready?"

His brother nodded.

"One. Two. Three…"

Gabe pushed himself off the landing into the back of the truck, purposely pounding hard against the metal. The sound of his shoes hitting the flatbed reverberated like thunder. He dropped to the floor of the truck and then rolled toward the window, making himself as small as possible.

The back window of the truck exploded as a shot hit the glass.

Gabe covered his head and his ears, praying the distraction had worked.

"I've got Calder," Ben said. "We're in the elevator going to street level. Are you okay?"

"I'm fine. He can't reach me unless he gets out of the truck."

Suddenly, the pickup truck jerked to life.

"Whoa," Gabe murmured.

Smith backed up and then slammed the brakes.

Gabe braced his legs and arms against either side of the vibrating metal of the bed, using all his strength to keep from bouncing out of the truck. At the same time, he prayed for an opportunity to pull out his weapon.

Smith floored it, shooting the vehicle forward. The sound of a spray of bullets indicated Smith hadn't forgotten his primary target. The BMW.

Then he backed up and did a one-eighty. Metal crunching metal drowned out squealing tires as Smith continued to hit parked cars as he headed back to the entrance. Burnt rubber filled Gabe's nostrils.

He dared to lift his head and peek over the side of the flatbed to where the minivan blocked the entrance.

Why did he think that was a good idea?

"Brace yourself, Mac. He's going to plow past the minivan."

"I've got this, Gabe." Her voice in his earbud was steady.

A single shot rang out.

"Mac!" Gabe's heart thudded as adrenaline shot through him. *Not Mac. Please, Lord. Not Mac.*

The truck swerved, the left rear bumper tagging the minivan before it crashed into the cement divider. Gabe slid forward and then bounced back against the tailgate.

Then the truck stopped.

"He's down," Mac said. The words were low and flat.

Gabe jumped out the back and staggered toward the minivan, then dropped to a knee. Relief was bittersweet. Another person dead. But Mac... Mac was alive.

"Are you all right?" Mac's breath was warm on his face. She slipped an arm beneath his and helped him to his feet.

"Yeah. I'm good. My equilibrium is pretty messed up, from bouncing around back there, but I'm okay."

"I'm glad," she said.

"Me, too." He met her gaze and smiled. "Very glad."

"What happened?" Ben asked through the bud in Gabe's ear.

"Smith is dead," he returned.

"What a waste." Ben sighed.

"What's happening with Calder?" Gabe asked.

"He's safe. We'll meet you in his condo. Second floor. Number twelve. Take the front entrance on Broadway. The door code is twenty-eight thirteen. He's kindly offered to host our next get-together."

"Nice job, Ben," Gabe said.

"Thanks. Would this be a good time to mention Denton Security and Investigations again?" his brother asked.

"No, it's not." Gabe went to the truck and checked for a pulse. Then he pulled up Smith's left sleeve. The lion tattoo, as Mac had described it.

He walked back to her. "Smith is your Toronto shooter. Lion tattoo, left arm. We should call Shipman. He'll send a team in to clean this up."

"Already called him." There was a tremor in her voice and her face was pale.

"Are you okay?" Gabe asked.

She wordlessly shook her head and glanced back at the truck. "I didn't want to do that," she whispered.

He pulled the Bluetooth from his ear and tucked it into his pocket. Then he wrapped his arms around her and pulled her close. "I know, Mac. I know."

"Morrow sent her shooter after you, Calder. Give her up," Gabe said. Calder grimaced, but said nothing.

Mac assessed the rogue agent from her position against the wall. Was that grimace a confirmation of Gabe's accusation, or of Liz's death on the pier? He wasn't cooperating and she might never know. Mac tucked her shaking hands under her crossed arms. She hadn't stopped trembling since she'd fired the Glock in the parking lot. The loss of life on this mission staggered her, and would for a long time.

Calder turned his head in Mac's direction and stared at her for a moment, his eyes unreadable, before he turned away. There was no malice. No, instead she thought she saw a glimpse of pity, which only confused her.

"Don't look at her," Gabe said. "I'm the one asking the questions."

"I have nothing to say, Officer Denton."

Gabe shrugged. "Fine. Homeland Security is on the way."

The agent sat in a wooden chair at his kitchen table, his hands restrained with flex-cuffs Mac found at the bottom of her messenger bag.

Gabe had been asking questions for thirty minutes and Calder had yet to respond. He knew his rights. They couldn't even arrest him, let alone persuade him to talk. Calder held tight to the knowledge that CIA agents have no law-enforcement authority in the United States. They'd have to wait for DHS to arrive.

Mac glanced around the room. "What happened to Ben?"

"He slipped out to talk to the car-rental place." Gabe raised his eyebrows. "Two rentals in less than a week. Ouch."

She nodded. They hadn't done any better. A total of four vehicles since leaving Phoenix last Friday.

Mac walked around the living room, unable to relax. The intimate kiss she'd observed at the airport between Calder and Liz told her that Liz had no doubt been here many times. A quick check of the condo when they arrived had revealed no evidence of her presence. Still, the place made Mac uncomfortable, almost nauseated. She had to get out soon.

"When can we leave?" she asked Gabe.

"When Shipman gets here."

"If Calder doesn't talk, what is he going to be charged with?"

"Treason. He knowingly altered CIA files. Shipman has no doubt already tracked his computer access. That should be enough to make him decide to talk."

A knock at the door had Gabe tensing, on alert again.

Mac's phone buzzed and she pulled it out of her pocket. "It's okay. It's Shipman and Homeland Security. He sent me a text."

Gabe opened the door, and Todd Shipman entered with two DHS agents.

"Nice work, Sharp, Denton."

"Thank you, sir," Gabe said.

"I've promised our friends at DHS that the two of you and your brother will make time to return and provide written statements. All standard procedure. Tomorrow work for you?"

"Yes, sir."

"Good." He handed Mac a set of keys. "I understand you like minivans. There's one parked at the curb. It's a rental. Keep that in mind when you return it to us in the same condition."

She tried not to smile. "Yes, sir."

They were silent on the elevator down to the ground floor. When they got in the minivan, Mac released a long breath, relieved to be on the way home to Winston.

"Do you think Calder will cooperate?" she asked. "He does have some leverage because there are still a lot of unanswered questions." She said the words more for herself than anything else.

Gabe nodded. "You're right. A lot of answers that went to the grave with Smith, Masterson and Ribinoff. We don't even know what happened to the money."

He signaled and merged into expressway traffic.

Mac's eyes were on the road ahead, and she didn't even notice the mountains to the west or the trees lining the roadway. Her thoughts were on Liz Morrow. They hadn't found her. Had she gone off the grid, was she being held by someone intent on finding the missing money, or was she dead?

"Calder was arrested. Smith is dead. Yet we still don't know anything about Liz." Her heart pounded in her chest as she spoke.

"Whoa, Mac, take a deep breath. It's going to be okay." Gabe reached out to hold her hand and squeezed gently.

"Is it?" Mac asked. "I've been in limbo for eight weeks…" She did a mental calculation. "Almost nine now. When will this nightmare end?"

ELEVEN

"Good boy, Winston." Mac caught her breath as she walked up the gravel drive to the log-cabin rental. While Ben and Gabe went to pick up the Thai food for dinner, she had gone for a stroll with the bulldog to clear the cobwebs from her mind.

She'd walked a little farther today. Not as fast as Winston preferred, but she was making progress.

Despite walking with a cane, her steps were lighter knowing the shooter who'd followed her for weeks was no longer a threat.

This morning, she, Ben and Gabe had provided their statements to DHS. There was no new intel on Liz, and so far, Calder hadn't cooperated with the authorities.

She couldn't hide forever. Maybe it was time to accept the fact that Liz was dead and move on. That meant Gabe would return to DC. Her steps slowed at the thought and emotion clogged her throat.

Mac reached in her pocket for her key to the

cabin. As she did, Winston stopped and sniffed, then growled low and deep. Pay attention to Winston. That's what Gabe said.

Out of habit, she patted the Glock tucked in her ankle holster. She could reach it quickly if needed.

"Lord, be with me," she prayed before unlocking the door.

Winston growled again as they walked into the entryway, where Mac held his collar with one hand, her cane with the other. "Sit." The dog whined, but obeyed.

"Hello, Mackenzie."

Mac whirled around and a jolt of adrenaline raced through her at the voice. Liz Morrow's voice.

Across the room, Liz sat on a stool drinking coffee from one of the cabin's mugs. A Glock rested on the counter within reach.

"You certainly are a lot of trouble." Liz smiled.

"Liz." Confused, Mac searched the woman's face for answers. But Liz merely cocked her head and assessed Mac in return.

"I've been waiting for hours for your friends to leave," Liz said. "Now it's just you and me."

A shiver ran over her as she confirmed that her guilt had been misplaced. Liz hadn't been kidnapped, and certainly wasn't dead. Her heart pounded in her ears and her chest tightened as she looked at the Glock on the counter again.

Nine weeks, and Liz was lovelier than ever. The dark hair tumbled to her shoulders and she seemed fit and healthy. She certainly hadn't suffered any sleepless nights.

"Nothing to say?" Liz taunted.

"What do you want me to say, Liz?" Mac fought to control her breathing and push back the fear. She wouldn't give her the satisfaction of a response.

"You could start by apologizing, dear Mackenzie. You spoiled everything."

"Did I?" Mac asked. "Why didn't you take the money and run?"

"Because you knew. You knew enough to connect me to the crime. When you blathered on in Toronto, I realized you had to go, so my plan could play out. I won't let you keep me from my spoils. I earned that money."

"Blood money?" Mac returned, spurred by outrage. So many had died because of Liz's greed.

Liz narrowed her eyes. "I hear that disdain in your voice. Spoken like a woman who knows nothing about growing up without anything. Not a name, not a past, a present or a future. Nothing. You will never understand what it's like to be alone in this world. To have all your worldly possessions fit into a paper bag from the grocery store."

"Oh, I know what it's like to be alone. We really aren't all that different."

"We have nothing in common," Liz sneered.

"Sure we do. Except you killed innocent people, Liz."

She raised a shoulder in dismissal. "All for the greater good."

"Shipman knows," Mac said. "And Calder is already in custody."

"Blake will never give me up. That leaves you. The key witness. Anything else is hearsay and conjecture. There isn't a shred of evidence." She grinned. "I'm that good."

Mac's stomach heaved at the words.

Liz glanced at her watch. Then she eyed Mac again. "How's the leg?" She shook her head. "My apologies. He was supposed to kill you. Not maim you."

Mac gripped her cane tightly.

"You look like you're in pain. Why don't you have a seat over there, in front of the window? I want you to be able to see me shoot your boyfriend, and that's a good spot."

"Go ahead and shoot me now. Denton isn't part of this."

"Maybe not, but you've managed to take almost everything from me in the last week. I'm going to return the favor."

Mac moved toward the rocker, her grip tight on the cane. Her pulse raced and her mind continued a desperate scramble for a plan.

"Wait," Liz called out.

Mac froze.

"Put your weapon on the floor and kick it over to me."

Mac released a breath. Liz was one of the few people who knew she had an ankle holster. She withdrew her Glock and kicked it toward Liz. Then she began to turn again.

"No. Don't move."

"You're going to shoot me in the back?"

"Of course not. Only a coward shoots someone in the back." She smiled. "I thought I heard something. But I guess I was wrong." Liz waved a hand toward the chair. "Sit. Sit. Get comfy."

Mac rocked slowly, her gaze taking in the landscape. Beside her, Winston sat watchful, as if waiting for permission to strike.

Liz Morrow was absolutely going to kill her. There was no trace of ambivalence in her voice. Only determination. If she could get her to talk, maybe she could distract her.

"So Calder was the one who planned everything, I assume."

Liz's eyes widened and she offered a bitter laugh. "Calder? He doesn't have the brains to plan an operation like that. I've been planning for two years. Two years. Bit by bit, so as not to call attention to myself or anyone else. Everything orchestrated down to the moment I dove off that pier."

"Calder's statement indicated the opposite," Mac lied.

"He's lying to you. I'm the brains. Calder doesn't know enough to tell anyone anything.

Everyone gets a piece of the information pie. No one but me gets the whole pie."

"I guess you managed to hide the money as part of your plan," Mac said.

"You'll never know, will you?" Liz shook her head, dark eyes glittering with anger.

Winston tensed at the rising tone of Liz's voice. He got to his feet and paced back and forth across the living room, ears perked, listening.

"Mackenzie, get the dog to settle down, or I'll shoot him."

Winston barked, confused, looking to Mac for direction.

"I mean it."

"It's okay, boy," she soothed. Though it wasn't. Nothing was okay.

Minutes ticked by. The window was open, but all Mac could hear was the splash of a duck on the pond, its wings flapping as it flew from the mirrored surface, into the sky.

Again, Liz looked at her watch. "What's taking him so long? I have a private jet waiting on me. The captain agreed to stow me aboard for a nominal fee." Once again she offered a satisfied smile. "Money can buy anyone and anything."

"Where are you going?" Mac asked.

"Montenegro. Did you know they don't have an extradition treaty with the United States?" She grinned. "Of course you didn't. It's beautiful. Quiet secluded beaches. The perfect place to become permanently invisible. And without you, I won't even have to look over my shoulder."

"It sounds lovely. Going alone?"

Liz laughed. "Look at you, trying to get intel from me. Maybe you should call your boyfriend instead. If he doesn't get here soon, I'm going to have to move on to Plan B. Not nearly as much fun."

"Why wait for Denton?" She stared at Liz, trying to understand what drove the woman.

"I told you. It's payback time." A faint smile touched her mouth. "Go ahead. Call him," Liz insisted.

"I don't have a phone. He took it with him." Mac eyed her messenger bag on a peg next to the door.

"I knew you were going to be a problem." Liz turned and reached for her cell phone on the counter.

When she did, Mac jumped from the rocker and grabbed her cane. She swung, and the metal rod connected with Liz's head with a thud and a crack.

Liz moaned and fell to her knees, swaying. "I'm going to kill you for that."

"Not if I can help it," Mac muttered. She grabbed her messenger bag and pulled open the door. "Come on, Winston."

The dog followed.

"Good boy. Now all I have to do is hobble faster than I have in my life."

* * *

"Do you hear that?" Gabe asked. He glanced around the floor of Ben's rental. A luxury vehicle, it was a dozen steps up from the minivan Shipman rented him and Mac yesterday.

"Buzzing," Ben said, his eyes on the road.

"My phone is in here somewhere."

"We're five minutes from the cabin. You can find it when we get there. Do I need to remind you that this is my third rental since I landed in Colorado? I'm keeping my eyes on the road and the vehicle away from criminal elements." Ben cleared his throat. "Speaking of the cabin. Maybe we should talk about what's next before we get there."

"Next? What do you mean?"

"It's Thursday. Calder has been arrested. What's next?"

"Oh, that next." Gabe nodded. He'd been asking himself the same thing. "I've reached out to Shipman to find out if he's gotten any intel on the Elizabeth Morrow situation. But nothing yet."

"Calder isn't talking."

Gabe shrugged. "Guess not."

"Let's chat with Mackenzie about it, and we can go from there," Ben said.

"I'm putting 'chat with Mac' on my schedule." The buzzing sounded again. "Can you pull over? This is annoying me. Could be something important. Maybe Shipman is trying to reach me."

Ben signaled and moved to the shoulder of the road. "I'll help you look. Just be gentle with the vehicle."

Gabe lifted the mats from the back seat with no results, then stuck his hand under the passenger seat and hit a rectangular object. "Found it." He got back in the car and put on his seat belt.

"Is it Shipman?" Ben asked.

"No—voice mail." Gabe pulled up his text messages and read the brief message from Mac. A guttural sound slipped from his lips, and he grimaced at the sucker punch that knocked the air from his lungs.

"You okay? What is it, Gabe?"

"Morrow is alive and she's at the cabin intent on eliminating Mac." Fear wrapped its hands around his neck and squeezed.

"She's alive?" Ben gripped the steering wheel. "What do you want to do?"

"Look, is that Winston?" Gabe pointed across the field adjacent to the cabin.

"Sure is," Ben said.

"Then Mac must be close by. Stop here, Ben. Let's ditch the car and approach on foot."

"Will do," Ben said. He guided the sedan off the road and pulled out his phone. "Sound is off. I must have turned it off accidentally. I've got those cameras on the cabin." He tapped the app and then the front-door feed, and checked the image captures. "Nothing out of the ordinary in front.

The capture shows Mac and Winston entering the cabin."

"Do you have a camera on the back door?" Gabe asked.

"Yeah." When an image capture of a woman appeared on the screen, Gabe grabbed the phone.

"Ben, isn't that Morrow? You saw the file photos."

"Yeah. That's her. She's got a Glock in one hand, and…" He paused. "Whoa. That's Mac coming out the door. And look at the next image. Morrow. She's leaning sideways. I'd say she's injured."

"How did she get to the cabin? I don't see a vehicle." Gabe pulled out his binoculars and did a 360-degree sweep. Lots of trees. No vehicles.

"I don't see one, either," Ben said. "She must have parked to the north and come in on foot."

"Let's go," Gabe said.

"What's your plan?" Ben asked.

"If only I had one." The only plan he had right now was to keep the promise he'd made to himself to protect Mac. His stomach burned when he thought about Morrow's deadly determination.

"Take comms," Ben said. "Morrow is armed, and we can't be sure Mackenzie is."

"Good idea." Gabe reached in his pocket for his Bluetooth.

"Gabe, look at me."

"Yeah?" He met Ben's gaze and drew a deep breath at the concern on his brother's face.

"You're going to be useless to Mackenzie if you let your emotions get in the way. You're a trained operative. This is a mission. Focus."

Gabe nodded, grateful for the words of wisdom. "You're right. I know you're right."

"Okay. Now, let's split up and take Morrow down," Ben said.

"Now you're speaking my love language. Why don't you come around the other side of the house?"

Gabe pulled his binoculars from his pocket again and searched the landscape around the lake, hoping to see Mac. Her leg injury would slow her down, and Morrow's bullet would find its target if she tried to outrun the rogue agent.

Mac was one of the smartest people he knew. She'd hide. That's what he'd do.

Now all he had to do was figure out where.

Winston raced back and forth along the trail around the lake. Protected behind the wide base of a blue spruce, Gabe released a low whistle, as soft as he dared, without alerting Morrow. The bulldog's ears perked up, and he looked around. Gabe stepped out, and the dog saw him and came running.

"Good boy," he soothed. "Now, where's Mac?"

"It's clear on this side of the cabin," Ben said. "I can see into the living room from the side window. No sign of Morrow or Mackenzie, but there's blood outside the back door."

Gabe's heart lurched at that information. "We know Morrow is injured. I pray Mac isn't also."

A gunshot rang out. Gabe froze in place, trying to determine the direction of the sound. But the geese scattering on the pond drowned out every other sound with their angry honks and flapping wings as they dispersed.

"Someone is shooting at us," Ben said in Gabe's ear.

"Where did that come from?" Gabe asked.

"Other side of the lake," Ben said. "I'll take the trail from the east."

"Come on, Winston." Gabe kept a close eye on the dog as they took the west side of the lake.

Another bullet whizzed by. This time, much too close. He couldn't risk Winston taking a bullet. Gabe slipped between the branches of a blue spruce and pulled Winston into the tree with him. The dog whined in protest.

"I don't like it, either, pal." He tapped his earbud. "Where are you, Ben?"

"To your right, behind that oak."

From the corner of his eye, Gabe saw a flash of light. He reached for his binoculars and swept the landscape. There it was. A flare. Right in front of a thicket of tall blue spruce.

Mac carried flares in her messenger bag. Why would she throw out a flare, which would only put a target on her location?

"I have eyes on Morrow," Ben said. "She's

moving toward that flare. Weapon still in her hand."

"I see her," Gabe said. "She'll pick us off if we get any closer."

"Where did the flare come from?" Ben asked.

"It's got to be Mac. We don't have a plan, but it seems she does."

A scream cut through the quiet. Then a gunshot.

"Go, Ben! I'll meet you at that flare."

"Come on, Winston." Gabe picked up speed, racing around the lake to the apex. From a distance, he could see two women fighting. Mac had her cane across Morrow's shoulders, pinning her down.

Gabe's relief was immediate. *Go, Mac.*

Ben came running around the corner a moment later. He stopped short and blinked as if he couldn't believe his eyes.

"Not that she needs us," Gabe said, "but let's give her a hand."

The two of them subdued Morrow's legs while Mac used flex-cuffs to restrain the woman's hands.

Gabe grabbed Liz by her clothing and pulled her to her feet. An angry Elizabeth Morrow lunged toward Mac. Winston growled, threatening to attack.

"Get that dog away from me," Morrow screamed.

Ben stepped forward, his weapon trained on the rogue agent. "Give me an excuse, lady."

"Winston. Come," Mac called. The bulldog immediately obeyed, returning to her side.

"How did you get the jump on Morrow?" Gabe cocked his head and stared at Mac. Even injured, she was a force to be reckoned with.

"Literally." Mac pointed to the tree next to them. "I climbed the tree. Tossed the flare and then jumped her."

"You climbed a tree with your leg?" Gabe glanced up through the dense branches of the tree in disbelief.

Mac dusted the dirt and pine needles from her clothes before she looked at him. "It was either that or die. I'm not ready to die."

"The gunshot I heard?" Gabe asked.

"It went off when Liz hit the ground. Fortunately, I wasn't hit."

"Whose blood was that on the porch?" Ben asked.

"Liz's. I hit her with my cane and took off."

Gabe continued to shake his head, amazement warring with pride. "How's your leg now?"

"It's fine. I landed with my weight on my right foot and my fist in her stomach."

He nodded, still stunned that she'd taken down the mastermind of a bank heist and the puppet master who'd manipulated at least four men to do her bidding.

"So basically, you didn't need us," Gabe said.

Mac looked up at him. "Oh, Gabe. I'll always need you."

Ben started laughing. "Mackenzie Sharp, you're okay."

Gabe shook his head. He had to agree with his brother. Mac was more than okay.

TWELVE

Mac sat down in a chair facing Senior Officer Todd Shipman's desk and waited for him to arrive. She propped her cane against her legs and wiped her moist palms on her black dress pants. The spacious office had multiple framed awards and degrees on the wall. Her gaze stopped at a simple wall calendar.

Monday again. So much had happened in a mere eleven days. Her life would never be the same. After today, that would be truer than ever.

"Sorry to keep you waiting." Todd Shipman entered the room and closed the door.

"Good morning, sir." She moved to stand, but he was quick to wave a hand.

"Don't get up." He took a seat behind his massive desk and offered a welcoming smile that helped Mac relax.

She couldn't help but note that her father would have been the same age if he was alive. Perhaps with the same gray that now dominated Todd Shipman's hair.

Don't look back, her mind warned. *Don't look back.*

"The Agency let you down, Mackenzie." Shipman released a breath. "I let you down." He steepled his fingers and grimaced as if in physical pain. "I'm sorry. More than I can express."

"I don't blame you. I should have seen beneath Liz's facade."

"You can't blame yourself. We were all fooled."

Mac shook her head. So much loss because of Elizabeth Morrow.

"The Director has already initiated a full investigation," Shipman said. "Protocols were in place, and yet both Calder and Morrow managed to misdirect and bypass procedure. It should have never happened."

"What will happen to Calder?"

"He's agreed to a deal and has implicated Morrow. His career is over, but I can't say what will happen next."

Mac digested that information. "And Morrow?"

"DHS is still working on the charges against her. Interestingly enough, the money hasn't been found."

Mac shook her head at the irony. Liz would be in jail for a very long time, unable to enjoy the money, wherever it was.

"I assume you're going to be able to finish rehabilitation on your leg, and then you'll be back with us," Shipman said.

"Rehab starts again this week. I hope to see more of you and Mary and the kids in the future," Mac said.

"I can start you on desk duty if you like?"

She took a deep breath. There was no need to hesitate, the decision had been thought out and prayed over. "Sir, I'm not returning to the Agency."

He frowned in confusion. "What am I missing here?"

Mac pulled an envelope out of her messenger bag. "I'm submitting my resignation. Effective today."

Shipman's face reflected surprise. "You're one of our best operations officers. You have a bright future."

"Thank you, but I'm ready for a new direction for that future."

"I see." He offered a slow nod as though processing the information. "Have you considered a career as an analyst? We have an opening for a technology-and-weapons analyst in Los Angeles."

"With all due respect, sir, it's time to walk away. Don't think I don't appreciate everything you've done for me."

"Nothing was done out of obligation, Mackenzie. It was because you're someone that I can rely on. I never had to think twice when you were on assignment. You've always been a valuable asset to the company."

She bowed her head. He wasn't making it any easier. "Thank you for that."

"If you'll be seeing the family more often, does that mean you're staying in Colorado?"

"Yes. I love Colorado. I'm going to find a house in the country so Winston can run. I'll spend time catching up on my reading and maybe do a little fishing." Just saying the words brought a smile to her lips.

"There's always a place for you at our table, metaphorically and literally." He leaned back in his chair. "Megan is home from college for a few more weeks. We'd love to have you for dinner this Sunday."

"Thank you."

"I'll tell Mary and the kids. They'll be delighted."

Mac stood and offered her hand, but Shipman shook his head. He came around his massive desk and embraced her. "You're a civilian now, Mackenzie. Family. I can hug you."

Mac choked back emotion at the embrace.

Yes. Family. It was time to let people in, as Gabe had reminded her.

Mac picked up her cane and started toward the door.

"Mackenzie."

She turned. "Sir?"

"Your parents would be so proud of you."

When she met Todd Shipman's gaze, his eyes were moist. Her heart swelled with emotion. "Thank you. That means so much."

He nodded and returned to his seat. "Would you send Denton in for me?"

Denton? She hadn't seen him since Thursday. The last few days had been a whirlwind of being debriefed and medical examinations.

"Yes, sir," she returned.

Gabe waited outside, chatting with Shipman's new assistant, a leggy blonde. The woman smiled up at him, and Mac couldn't help a tiny twinge of longing. There wasn't anyone Gabe couldn't strike up a conversation with.

She'd had her chance once. There was no reason for regrets.

Mac cleared her throat. When he turned in her direction, she nodded toward Shipman's office and he offered a quick nod of acknowledgement in return. As Gabe passed by her, he touched her arm and paused. "Did you drive here?"

"Um, no. I took a ride-share. I was running late and didn't want to deal with parking."

"Wait for me. I'll give you a lift home."

She opened her mouth to protest, but he spoke before she could, his hazel eyes warm with entreaty.

"Please."

"Sure," she said softly. "I'll be outside."

Mac didn't do goodbyes. They hurt, and saying goodbye to this man wouldn't be easy. Not when he'd managed to bluster his way past all her objections and convince her heart that she was capable of trusting…and loving.

Yes, Gabe Denton deserved a few minutes of her time before they went their separate ways.

Mac took the elevator to the lobby and nodded to the guards before pushing open the glass doors. She stood on the sidewalk, letting the sunshine warm her face, watching morning traffic and busy people with places to be hurry past. Life continued to move on as though nothing had happened.

Her phone vibrated, and she checked the screen. It was a text message from Mary Shipman.

Todd says you're joining us for dinner on Sunday. I'm so glad.

Mac laughed. It had been all of ten minutes, and already Shipman had given his wife Mac's new phone number and told her about their conversation.

Thanks, Mary. I can't wait.

And she couldn't. It would be good to see the Shipmans. She was moving on, but that was okay. It was time. Time to make peace with the past and begin to carve out a future.

She'd spent years feeling guilty because she hadn't died with her parents in the embassy bombing, instead of appreciating the fact that she was alive.

Thankful.

That was the word that popped into her spirit. Mac smiled. Very thankful.

"Ready?" Mac turned at the sound of Gabe's voice behind her. He stood there blocking out the sun, yet she felt warm in his presence.

"What are you looking at?" Gabe asked. "It's the clothes, right?" He glanced down at his dress shirt and pants. "You haven't seen me in anything that wasn't wrinkled, torn or bled on since I arrived."

"You look very nice," Mac said. "And your bruises are fading. How are your ears? Have you had your hearing evaluated?"

"I'm cleared to fly." He grinned. "The doc says I made a wise decision to drive from Phoenix."

"Yes, you're very wise." Mac couldn't help but laugh.

He nodded toward the left. "Car's parked around the corner."

"I thought you had a coveted parking pass," Mac said.

"I'm leaving. Had to turn it in."

"Right." Another reminder that he'd be gone soon.

They walked to a black SUV, not unlike the one

that exploded in Phoenix, and he held the door for her before getting in.

"Rental?" she asked.

"Yeah." He turned in his seat to look at her. "We've come full circle, haven't we?"

Mac smiled. "Yes. I guess we have."

Gabe put on his seat belt and gestured toward Mac's leg. "Any issues with medical for you?" he asked.

"No. I'll be back in rehab tomorrow."

"Then what?" he pressed.

"I've got that inheritance from my parents. I've been thinking about buying a little land."

"A little island?"

She laughed. "No. A little parcel of land. Something with enough room for Winston to run. Maybe out in Larkspur. Despite the past week."

"That's a long commute."

"No." She shook her head. "Sorry. I wasn't clear. I'm not going back to the Agency. I'm done. I want to taste normal."

"Normal. Is that really what you're looking for?"

"I'm not sure. But it's a start."

"You're seriously leaving the CIA?" Gabe slowly shook his head. "What will you do?"

Mac shrugged. "Maybe I'll do nothing for a while. Nothing sounds really good."

"Don't forget. You owe me a fly-fishing trip. I'll expect an email regarding your availability soon."

She smiled once more. It was good to be able to joke with Gabe. She'd missed their repartee the last few days.

"You're the one who still has a job," she answered. "Let me know when you have time off."

"Oh, I will."

"What about your day job, anyhow?" Mac asked. "Promotion finalized?"

"Yeah. I'll be back at The Farm in time for the incoming recruits."

"Great. I'm sure you're good at your job. You have a lot of patience."

"Do I?" He glanced at her.

"Yes," she returned. "What about Ben?"

"Back to DC. We're flying out together this afternoon."

"You're still not interested in joining Denton Security and Investigations?" She peeked at him from the corner of her eye. It was too much to hope he'd stay in Denver and join the family business.

"Oh, yeah. I'm definitely interested. My heart says yes." He paused. "But my head is wavering."

"I can relate. That's what took me so long to decide to leave the Agency. Stepping out into the unknown is never easy."

"Look at you, talking all philosophical," Gabe said.

"I'm not being philosophical. What I'm trying

to say is your brother's company sounds like a great future. I think your father will be proud."

"That's because you don't know the general." He started the car, turned on the AC and drummed his fingers on the steering wheel as the cool air blew in. "I'm a coward."

"I didn't say that."

"No. I did."

He backed up the SUV and headed down Santa Fe. Mac kept sneaking looks at Gabe as they drove in silence to her condo. When would she see him again? Five years? Ten? What regrets would she have then?

"I never noticed that dog park before." Gabe signaled and pulled up to the drop-off area in front of her building.

"It's fairly new. The city added it a few years ago. I guess they knew Winston was coming to live with me."

"He likes it?"

"Loves it. We're there several times a day."

Gabe nodded, a smile touching his mouth. "I'm going to miss you and Winston."

Mac looked out the window. She didn't know how to say the words that were locked inside of her. How could she possibly ask him to stay?

"We're going to miss you, too, Denton."

"Are we back to that?" He cocked his head and gave her a censuring look.

"Gabe." She reached for the door handle, looked at him, and then away. "Gabe, I..."

"What?" he asked.

"Thank you. For everything."

She opened the door and carefully stepped onto the sidewalk, using her cane to keep her steady, though she felt anything but steady right now.

"Be safe," Mac said before turning away.

Because I care for you. I always will.

Gabe verified his departure time on the flight-information display and wandered to a bookstore. His phone buzzed, and he pulled it out.

A text from his brother.

In TSA line. Join you shortly.

Disappointment hit Gabe.

What was he expecting? Mac to call and beg him to stay?

Yep, that was exactly what he wanted. Waited his whole life for. Mac was his future, but she couldn't see it. Maybe never would.

A quick stroll around the bookstore proved fruitless. After nearly bumping into several harried customers in a rush to get in and out, he left. The truth was, he didn't need a book or a magazine.

He needed Mac.

Gabe headed back to the gate. Walking down

the long corridor, he spotted Ben and waved his arms. Ben jogged to meet him.

"Thought I was going to miss the flight."

"Where were you?" Gabe asked.

"Pacing the parking lot and arguing with the insurance company. Do you know how hard it is to explain that your vacation rental was destroyed by a rogue government operative and get someone to believe you?"

Gabe's head jerked up at the words. "Naw. Tell me you didn't say that."

Ben laughed. "I didn't, but all the same, it was time-consuming."

Overhead a speaker crackled, and the first boarding announcement rang out.

"I take it Shipman booked us first class," Ben said.

"Keep dreaming," Gabe said with a laugh. "It's good to have dreams. The boarding pass indicates we're in the last row, next to the restroom."

Ben groaned. "That means I sit with my knees under my chin for four hours." His brother cocked his head and looked him up and down. "What are you doing on this flight, anyhow?"

"What do you mean?"

"Why are you leaving Denver?"

"Because I have a job in DC. Any other silly questions?" Gabe leaned against the wall and frowned.

"Yeah, but Mackenzie is here." Ben narrowed his gaze. "And you're in love with her."

Gabe stared at his brother. He considered denying the accusation, but what would be the point? Ben saw far too much.

He released a sigh. "My being in love with Mac doesn't change the situation."

"Are you going to wait another five years before your paths cross and you have a third opportunity to do something?"

"Do something? Ben, I can't keep banging my head against the wall around her heart."

"Sure, you can. This is it, man. We all could have been killed at any time in the last week. No guts. No glory. No risk. No reward." Ben raised his hands. "How many more pithy quotes do I have to recite? Life is short, man."

"What if she doesn't...?"

"She loves you."

"How can you be sure? I'm never certain what Mac is feeling from one moment to the next."

"Trust me. It's in her eyes when she looks at you."

Gabe took a deep breath, as he considered his brother's words. Could Ben be right? He'd been waiting five years for her. Was it a foolish dream to think Mac might change her mind about them?

"I know that dog loves you. And if a woman's dog loves you, then the woman does, too."

"So I should try, one more time, because of a drooling one-hundred-pound bulldog?"

"That, and there's the fact that she called me and asked if I was still considering opening a Denver office."

"What? When was this?"

"On my way over." He shrugged. "She wants to invest her inheritance in the company."

"What?"

"You already said that."

"Pardon me, but I'm stunned."

"Yep. I was a bit surprised, too. My theory is that if Mac didn't want anything to do with the Dentons, she wouldn't have called."

"None of this makes any sense," Gabe said.

"It's love. It's not supposed to make sense."

Gabe narrowed his eyes. "How is it you're the expert?"

"I listen to a lot of podcasts when I'm on the road."

Gabe burst out laughing. Overhead, another boarding call was announced.

"They just called for all passengers seated next to the restroom," Ben said. "You better make a decision."

Gabe glanced at the lines of people funneling past the gate agent. "I guess I could always get a later flight if she says no."

His brother grinned and gave him a thumbs-up.

"That's the indomitable Denton optimism. Mom would have been proud."

"Thanks, Ben."

"Sure. I'd expect you to kick me in the seat of my pants if the situation was reversed."

Gabe gave his brother a man-hug. "Seriously. No matter how this turns out, I appreciate you. I'm glad you're my brother."

He pivoted and headed back down the long corridor of the airline terminal. At the elevator bank, he punched the button for ground transportation. He'd already turned in the rental car. How was he going to get to Mac's place?

A cab. More expensive, but cabs would be lined up and waiting.

Warmth surrounded him as he passed from the air-conditioned doorway to the outside sidewalk. Another hot day. Though not as hot as Phoenix, he reminded himself. And certainly not as hot and humid as DC.

Denver was a nice town. Crossing the street to the cab station, his gaze took in the mountains to the west. God's country. He could see himself waking up to those mountains every day.

It all depended on Mac.

He found himself more terrified of her response than he'd been at that last standoff at the cabin. Except when he thought Liz had killed Mac.

That was a moment he never wanted to face again.

Gabe waved a cab over.

Ben was right. He'd never stopped loving Mackenzie Sharp.

Now he prayed she felt the same.

"Go get it, Winston," Mac called. The chew bone sailed across the grass, and the dog eagerly chased it. Right now, she was the only one at the dog park, so Winston had the luxury of being off his leash without being in the designated play area and he was enjoying himself. He jumped in the air and caught the toy, then rolled on the grass wrestling with it.

Mac glanced at her watch and then at the sky. It was almost dinnertime. Gabe would be on his way to DC by now. She swallowed. That was good. He got the promotion. Great for his career. She wouldn't be surprised if he was sitting behind a desk like Shipman's the next time they ran into each other. And he deserved it.

But where would she be when Gabe was getting on with his life without her?

Mac hadn't a clue. She had let Ben know that she was interested in Denton Security and Investigations if a Denver office panned out. Her college degree was in economics with a French-language minor. Maybe she'd teach. Maybe she'd take a trip to France.

There wasn't a rush to make a decision. She had a few weeks of physical therapy ahead of her.

Though even that looked promising. Despite the trauma of the last week, the orthopedic surgeon said her leg was healing well. He'd assured her that once she'd finished treatment, the cane most likely wouldn't be needed.

That thought cheered her up.

Winston picked up the chew toy and raced toward her.

And right on past.

"Winston? Where are you going?"

Mac whirled around. "Stop." She blinked, certain she was hallucinating. But, no, it really was Gabe striding across the grass in her direction. Winston kept running joyously toward him.

When Gabe crouched down, the dog leaped into his open arms and knocked him over. Winston began an enthusiastic inspection of Gabe's face with his tongue.

"Winston. Stop," she called. The animal ignored her.

Gabe raised himself to a seated position and adjusted his glasses. He chuckled as he rubbed Winston's head and ears.

"Hi, Mac," he said.

"Gabe? What are you doing here?"

"Good to see you, too." He lifted an eyebrow. "I guess you didn't miss me."

"I just saw you this morning." She checked her watch. "You're supposed to be on your way to DC."

"Missed my flight."

"Oh," she murmured. "I'm sorry."

"On purpose."

Mac's chin lifted, and she stared at him, confused. "What did you say?"

"Someone pointed out to me that taking a chance and being shot down was better than never taking a chance at all."

"Um…" She swallowed, her breath stuck in her throat. "I don't know what to say to that."

"Glad to hear it." Gabe nodded toward the bench. "Let's sit down."

He scooped up Winston's chew toy and pulled back his arm. The rubber toy sailed a distance twice as long as Mac had pitched it minutes before.

Mac sat on the bench and folded her hands on her lap, uncertain of the protocol here. Was this the part where she told him that she'd been the coward? Or the part where she begged him to stay?

"Here's the thing, Mac." Gabe sat and stretched out his long legs. "I'm in love with you."

"I—I…" she sputtered and worked to catch her breath.

"I know. I know. Imagine how surprised I was. But, when you think about it, it's not a surprise. When you find the right person…" He shrugged and sighed loudly. "Why keep looking? Right?"

Mac's knees trembled and goose bumps danced up her arms.

Gabe Denton just said he loved her.

She glanced at him, leaning back with his arm across the back of the bench.

How could he be so relaxed? This moment would define the rest of her life.

"So here's the thing," he continued. "I'm not willing to close the door on us a second time until you tell me that you don't love me."

"Um," she squeaked.

He raised a hand. "I'm not done yet. I practiced this speech on the way over, so you may as well let me get it out of my system."

"Okay," she murmured.

"The thing is, I don't think you can use that fear-of-someone-you-love-dying rationale for not living your life. Not after the last week. We both could have died. Several times. But we didn't. We made it, Mac."

He turned to her. "There are no guarantees. I'd rather live my no-guarantees life with you by my side than without."

"Me, too."

Gabe's eyes popped open. "I wasn't expecting that. I have at least two more persuasive arguments."

Mac smiled slowly. "You came prepared."

"Yeah, I did. I'm not letting you go this time."

"I love you, Gabe." The words came naturally. Probably because she'd wanted to say them for such a very long time.

"Oh, thank You, Lord," Gabe said. He closed

the space between them and then stopped and pulled back. He removed his holster and placed it on the bench.

Mac laughed as his lips met hers.

"Stop laughing so I can give you a proper kiss."

She wrapped her arms around his neck and complied, her lips meeting his for a sweet kiss.

"Looks like I can tell Ben we're opening a Denver office of Denton Security and Investigations."

Mac brightened. "You're going to stay in Denver?"

"Absolutely. Welcome to the family business, Mackenzie Sharp."

Winston whined and nosed his face between them. "You're part of the family, too, boy." Gabe leaned down and gave the bulldog a loving head rub.

"What happens next?" Mac asked.

"I'm starving," Gabe said. "How do you feel about sushi?"

Mac laughed. "I'll follow your appetite anywhere, Gabe Denton."

He leaned close, his breath warming her face. "I thank God for you, Mac. Every single day." And then he kissed her again.

* * * * *

If you enjoyed this book,
pick up these other exciting stories from
Love Inspired Suspense.

Defending from Danger
by Jodie Bailey

Texas Buried Secrets
by Virginia Vaughan

Cavern Cover-Up
by Katy Lee

Shielding the Tiny Target
by Deena Alexander

Hidden Ranch Peril
by Michelle Aleckson

Find more great reads at
www.LoveInspired.com

Dear Reader,

Thank you so much for picking up Gabe and Mackenzie's story. This book was such a treat to write. It was particularly satisfying because these characters have been in my head talking to me for a long time.

I love Gabe Denton's wonderful sense of humor and his outlook. Mackenzie (Mac) Sharp had such a journey to self-forgiveness and trust. Their story makes me sigh every single time.

I pray whatever journey you're on that you let someone in, as Gabe advised Mac. Above all, let the Lord in. The road may seem endless, but He'll never let you faint.

Tina Radcliffe